CW01512024

Rerun at Rialto

Tom Alter

Rerun at Rialto

VIKING

VIKING

Penguin Books India (P) Ltd., 11 Community Centre, Panchsheel Park, New Delhi 110 017, India
Penguin Books Ltd., 80 Strand, London WC2R 0RL, UK
Penguin Putnam Inc., 375 Hudson Street, New York, NY 10014, USA
Penguin Books Australia Ltd., Ringwood, Victoria, Australia
Penguin Books Canada Ltd., 10 Alcorn Avenue, Suite 300, Toronto, Ontario, M4V 3B2, Canada
Penguin Books (NZ) Ltd., Cnr Rosedale and Airborne Roads, Albany, Auckland, New Zealand

First published in Viking by Penguin Books India 2001

Copyright © Tom Alter 2001
Illustrations copyright © Shalini Agarwal

10 9 8 7 6 5 4 3 2 1

Typeset in *Sabon Roman* by SÜRYA, New Delhi
Printed at Chaman Offset Printers, New Delhi

Illustrations by Shalini Agarwal

1

WHEN I CAME round the last bend in the path and saw him there—standing in front of my uncle's bench, framed against the early-morning Mussoorie mist—I knew that I had found what I was searching for.

And as I rested against a pine for a moment, I also knew that another search—deeper, keener—had begun.

But first, like a good policeman, let me backtrack just a little.

—

It was a few minutes past 2 a.m. when I called Khanna in Mussoorie from the STD booth at Chhuttmalpur.

I had stopped at the row of dhabas along the Saharanpur road, picked out one that I thought—that I hoped—was the one where the good Colonel and I had dined on another winter night, thirty years ago, and ordered *kaleji*-fry, daal and rotis in the Colonel's honour. That dinner had come at the end of a blessed day of fishing on the Jamuna canal. We had shared so much—one good catch, army jokes, lunch with friends from Jagadhri, early December weather, late afternoon sunshine and slight sweat . . . Ah, but that is another story.

Chhuttmalpur lies at a crossroads—if you are coming from the plains, you can turn right for more plains, or carry on straight across the Shivaliks to Dehra Dun and Mussoorie and the hills.

I was coming from the plains. From Delhi, to be precise. I had spent the evening in a town where I had lived for a few years as a very small boy—a town filled with good memories, not only because it was the location for so many oft-heard childhood tales, but also because it lay on the way to the adventure and great outdoors of the Punjab.

Which made the restlessness, the weariness, of that evening all the deeper.

You see, every winter I take a month off, mount my old and faithful Jawa, and travel unannounced, in jeans and jacket, or faded tracksuit, from police station to police station, town to town, dhaba to dhaba. It is a time to grow a beard, recharge the batteries, discover life all over again (that is the hope, at any rate)—and, as an Inspector General of Police on the road, check up on what is really happening in this ever-changing world.

It used to be a special time for me, this winter break—a time I would build the rest of the year around.

Until, over the past few years, everything began to change.

I have always been able to deal with crime, with the ugly side of human nature, because I had a belief, a confidence, in the basic goodness of people, and the essentially sane fabric of our society. It may sound simplistic, but for me it was true. This belief gave me the strength to face almost anything. And if it ever began to weaken, I would run into people, or situations, that would breathe life back into it.

Till, as I said, some years ago. With disturbing and then depressing regularity, I began to no longer meet those people, or find those situations. Instead, a wall of indifference met me at every turn. As a very wise man once said, 'The opposite of love is not hate—it is indifference.'

And I kept asking myself—was it really our world that had become so indifferent, so corrupt, so cruel, or had something changed inside me? For the first time in my life, I grew restless and weary. It did not come upon me suddenly. It built up slowly, like an ache inside, even as I struggled to ignore it, and then to understand it. The life I had lived hadn't equipped me to handle this weariness, and before the start of this winter's travels, I found myself desperate for a balm, a healing touch, that would make me whole again.

I had hoped that the town of my early childhood would at least begin the healing process—not only because of the memories, but because a crucial case I was investigating depended on a key witness who lived in that town. He was the son of one of my late father's closest friends, and I was sure I could count on him to have the courage to tell the truth.

But the evening in that town—like too many other recent evenings in too many other towns—had been full of many questions and no answers. The key witness greeted me with a disarming smile and a warm hug, and asked after all the members of my far-flung family. But through the evening he very cleverly refused to even discuss the case, much less tell the truth. All this he did while offering me a sumptuous dinner and a place for the night, and glimpses into scrapbook evidence of our everlasting relationship.

He bade me farewell with another smile, another hug, and I drove into the cold, dark evening, more tired than I should have been. I spoke to total strangers; had tea with officers at the *thana*—discussing their lives and their problems; roamed the streets, checking out the film posters and the hoardings. Then I parked at a corner and listened and watched as the world bustled busily around me.

But to no avail. Only inconclusive evidence of physical, emotional and mental corruption filled the night. I did not know this place anymore. Everywhere, like ill-lit streets, were half-truths, not even the purity of lies.

The gist of a line from *Lawrence of Arabia* drifted up through my shifting, unsettled thoughts as I took the Jawa out of the clutches of the night and that town. 'People who speak lies at least know where the truth is; people who speak half-truths have forgotten where they put it.'

Or something close to that.

The onions and masala of the kaleji-fry, and memories of the Colonel—alas, now fishing the canals of a better world—almost cut through the restlessness.

But not quite.

When I went up to pay, the dhaba-wala refused to take any tip from me. Not because he recognized me as a famous IG, but because he remembered the Colonel and the Colonel's friends. He asked if I would be going up to Mussoorie. No, only up to Dehra Dun, I told him. I did not tell him that I hadn't been back to Mussoorie since that fishing trip. More than thirty years. I had come several times on work to towns like Chhuttmulpur, so close to those hills, and turned back.

Maybe it was the Colonel, with that sardonic wisdom of his, who convinced me to call Khanna in Mussoorie.

Anyway, at the STD booth near the crossroads, I did.

Khanna's wife answered the phone, and even before she spoke I heard a few bangles jangle sleepily as her deliciously plump arm, reaching out from the cocoon of a *razai* on a February night, brought the earpiece to rest against the sumptuous folds of her upper neck.

'Helloo?'

Her voice was as plump and sweet as the rest of her.

'*Bhabhi*, sorry to disturb you so late. This is Kohli here.'

'Allan? You!! The great IG Allan Kohli! Arre, you can disturb me whenever you like. Your dear friend the DSP never does.'

The laughter in her voice melted into her words, and suddenly I was delightfully, insanely jealous of Khanna.

'Be very careful what you offer to policemen, my dear. We're used to having our way.'

She answered with a ripple of laughter, and I was instantly reminded of juicy *jalebis* dipped in hot milk.

'If my dear friend is not bothering you on a cold winter's night in Mussoorie—as any sensible man should—then where is he?'

'Don't ask! Some rich *lalaji* from Delhi has lost his wife at Rialto cinema and is swearing he will wake up our Prime Minister and get your friend transferred to Bihar unless the missing wife is located immediately!'

'Missing from Rialto? I thought Rialto itself was missing!'

'Arre, baba, Rialto *was* missing, but it's been back in business for the past three years. If you would only come back to Mussoorie now and then, instead of constantly trying to solve all the world's problems, IG sahib, you might find out what is going on around here. What's missing now is lalaji's wife. And since your dear friend has not called home in the past two hours, I presume the lucky lady is still missing. If I were married to lalaji, I would also go missing!'

'You met him?'

'I heard him. That was enough. He came shouting into our house at about midnight, threatening to disturb our Prime Minister's sleep, and totally destroying ours instead.'

This time the ripple of laughter was like melting snow slipping off a red tin roof.

'And it wasn't just our sleep he destroyed. My happiness as well. Your friend was about to show his feelings for me after many a moon!'

'He will, Bhabhi, he will. And soon. Trust me. But tell me, how did this woman disappear?'

'So—now suddenly you're a policeman, and have forgotten about disturbing me! *Badmash*. Just like your friend. Now leave me alone, and call him at the thana. He will answer all your questions.'

'Bhabhi—I'm sorry.'

'Arre, I know, baba. And I still love you. And the DSP sahib, though sometimes I wonder. Just find yourself a wife. Then all will be well. Now call your friend. And *haan*, I didn't ask. Where are you calling from? Delhi?'

'Chhuttmalpur.'

'Chhuttmalpur? In the middle of the night? Then get on that silly toy of yours and get to Mussoorie as fast as you can. Are you going to stay away from here for ever? We are sick and tired of visiting you in Delhi, at those pathetic bachelor quarters of yours. Come here and I'll fatten you up and find you a wife.'

With a last jangle of her glass and gold bangles, she removed the reluctant phone from its nestling place, and put it out into the cold.

And I knew that I was on my way back to Mussoorie.

2

I THINK I saw him before he saw me.

Or perhaps he saw me from a long way off, yet wanted to give me the advantage of first sight, so that the meeting, the situation, would be in my control.

That's the way he is.

Always has been.

He was standing at the edge of the path, with my uncle's bench behind him, looking to the east, as if waiting for the morning sun to melt the mist.

He was stooped, just a little, but that certainty in his posture was still there—that strength through the legs, the slim ease of back and shoulder, the neck erect and yet at peace, the chin and nose like well-worn ridges on the proud, honest plains of his face. There were no questions in his pose, no restlessness for answers.

I had stopped about thirty yards down the path that leads up from Jabbarkhet towards our old family

house. The jog from the school gate to Jabbarkhet—so short and sweet in inter-school cross-country days—had left me more winded than I had anticipated.

I think he realized this, because when I called out his name, and he turned towards me, there was a smile on his face.

The same gentle, open smile with which he greeted Paul and me, young schoolboys on the verge of life's adventure, at the entrance to Rialto when we used to come charging from detention at school through the bazaar to catch the 11:00 a.m. English matinee on Saturdays. The same smile with which he used to sneak us, free of charge, into the magic darkness of Rialto, and after the show, offer us not only *aloo-tikkis* and Cokes, but also the quiet wisdom of his life.

Chandu.

How did he know that the first place I would come to in Mussoorie after thirty years would be my uncle's bench?

How would he not know?

For a long while we stood still and just looked at each other—now only thirty yards separating us—famished by memories, by all the years apart, by the song of the wind in the pines.

Then, sprinting, calling his name, I charged up the path.

Almost shyly, he opened his arms out to me slightly in greeting.

Only then did I notice, as my senses finally focused on the here and now, that his face was twisted down over his right eye.

—

I had left the Jawa at the police station in Rajpur, and requested that it be brought up to Mussoorie in the morning.

Rajpur lies right at the base of the Mussoorie slope, and the old walking path starts there. When my father went to school in Mussoorie as a young boy, he used to take this path because Rajpur was as far as the motor road went.

To honour his memory, and also because I love to walk, just as he did, I had chosen to return to Mussoorie on foot. I had promised Khanna that I would reach Rialto by 8 a.m., and it was only 4 a.m. when I started the climb up through Rajpur bazaar.

The ride from Chhuttmalpur to Rajpur—up and down the Shivaliks and then through a sleeping Dehra Dun and onto Rajpur Road, an arrow gliding towards the hills, had passed like a series of songs on an old Beatles album. Or from an old Rajesh Khanna film. Favourite lines, certain moments in the melody, rose effortlessly from the depths of my heart after many a musty year.

As the Jawa swung and swayed through the folds

of the Shivaliks—with the 'handkerchief of the headlight' (as my brother so wonderfully describes it) waving out at ancient bridges and sleeping river beds—my mind cut loose and drifted away into the darkness, fantasizing about the smooth breasts of women never loved, the sixes never struck, the soft melodies of songs never sung. Then it would come back suddenly home again on a steeper stretch of road, or a tight bend where the gears had to be changed. And I would ponder, almost reluctantly, on what Khanna had told me over the phone when I called him at the thana.

When the descent into Dehra Dun began, my mind broke free again. It was as if I was a rock star, possessed by my own performance, overcome by the sense of power and the throbbing rhythm. I was complete. No memories, no nostalgia, no fantasies. Just the speed of the bike and the chill of the wind and the earth flowing away like silk below me.

On Rajpur Road, though, I became Bob Dylan. It is a gentle climb, and the years drifted away to the music of 'Baby Blue' and 'Tambourine Man'. I was twelve years old, cycling home with my brother, his broad back showing the way.

People who think they know me well would be shocked at what I can become—at least in my fantasies—on a bike. But that night I shocked even myself with the intensity of my emotions.

Which was another reason why I wanted to walk up from Rajpur to Mussoorie. To ease my mind, even as I tested my legs. To give myself time to collect my thoughts and get a hold over the strong emotions filling my mind. To approach Mussoorie in a way least expected, so that my arrival, my return, would be my own.

And it worked. The first, steep climb up the gravelly trucking trails above Rajpur caught and winded me. But by the time I reached the level area beyond the old tea shop, my strides had found a nice, even rhythm, and my breathing began to settle.

Points of pilgrimage arrived en route like old friends. The narrow, green field of Oak Grove, just off the main road, slept in the quiet darkness; and the suspension bridge connecting St George's and the new five-star hotel hung overhead like a welcoming banner at Barlowganj. From there began the steep climb to the Allen School gate, and my head was so full of memories, it felt as though I was crossing through a field of heavily scented flowers. I stood awhile at the gate, the portal to sporting glory, as if at the memorial of a revered guru, before I began my ultimate pilgrimage— the descent into and crossing of the valley which separates Allen from my old school.

We used to make the journey—on the way to cricket matches or inter-school sports—in fifteen mad-dash minutes. But the new road, built in the years I was away, had forced the old path to find different, unfamiliar routes across the valley, which left me stumbling and falling and laughing at myself. But when I finally crossed the stream and began the heavily wooded climb up to the girls' hostel, the path rearranged itself for me in welcome. I was home.

I won't attempt to describe this climax of my odyssey. Nostalgia is too private a treasure, too delicate, and I've risked it enough already. Suffice it to say that upon reaching the girls' hostel, I heard voices, calling from the darkened windows, which I had not heard for decades, and I didn't have the courage to run down the path leading to the school field. By the time I reached the school gate, I was one with the wind and the trees and the cold and the darkness—so that when an old friend, a chowkidar who had known me since I was a kid, found me weeping at the gate, he said he had almost mistaken me for a shadow.

And it was as a shadow that I ran up Tehri Road to Jabbarkhet, and then turned up the path towards my uncle's bench, little knowing that my journey, so long delayed, would end before the one person who could fully understand it.

3

THE TWIST OF Chandu's face, over his right eye, made me pause for a moment, and he saw it. One hand touched his eyebrow in acknowledgement of the change, even as the other arm reached out to touch me. But not to embrace me. That is something Chandu would never do.

But I embraced him, as tightly as I could. His rough *pahari* jacket felt like a blanket, and I wanted to settle in and sleep forever.

When I finally pulled back, Chandu was looking straight into my eyes, which were filling up again.

Did he understand? Or did he feel that grown men like me should hold back their tears—as I had done for so long? I couldn't ask him, because that is not what men do. Instead, Chandu explained about his eye.

'Sahib, for more than forty years I have been checking tickets at Rialto. Thousands and thousands of tickets. And always with my right eye squinted over the torch. Do you remember? You used to tease me about it—and your friend Paul . . . What a badmash he was. So, slowly, my right eye just very nicely settled into a permanent squint. That's all.'

Those were probably the most words in a row Chandu had ever spoken. To me, or anyone else. Then there was silence. And in that silence, a deep peace settled inside me—a peace I had not felt in years.

It was several moments before Chandu spoke again.

'But it is amazing, sahib, you have hardly changed at all. Your hair has thinned a bit at the front, and your beard is greying, but otherwise you are still Allanbaba!'

How could I tell him that all I wanted now was to be Allan-baba for the rest of my life. To be next to him until the mist lifted and the Tehri Road appeared, like a ribbon on the gift of the hills, and then to look out into those familiar hills, never saying a word.

'Chandu, you are the one who hasn't changed. Look at you! You could still play half-back for Rock Blue on Survey Field.'

He chuckled. 'Sahib, you will have to convince Bamboo to let me play. He always listened to you.'

'I heard he joined politics. Like everyone else.'

'Oh, just a little. But he's still a sportsman at heart.'

'Like you and me.'

This silenced us both. We turned towards the mist.

In the cities, such silence can create tension. In the hills, it is a melody.

'And Rialto?' I finally asked. 'How's it doing? I hear it's open again.'

'Yes, sahib. All of Mall Road was in mourning when we had to close down. But we came back. We had to.'

'Thank goodness. Watching a film again at Rialto is what I dream about.'

'Really, sahib?' He was looking straight into my eyes. 'I thought policemen never had dreams.'

I waited for a chuckle, to be sure that he was pulling my leg. The chuckle came, but after a long moment, when even the wind in the pines was stilled.

'Oh yes we do, Chandu. We have to dream. It keeps us sane.'

'You say this, sahib? The great IG Allan Kohli— the biggest policeman in all of India? You know how proud we are of you, sahib? We keep telling each other that it's fine if Allan-baba never comes back to Mussoorie, because wherever he goes, whatever he does, he is making Mussoorie famous.'

I felt the tears again, and had to turn away.

'But we missed you, sahib. All of us. Brij and Ajay and Bamboo and Kapoor-sahib and Arora-sahib and Khanna-sahib and Kapadia-sahib—and so many others.

And sometimes we ask each other—just among ourselves—why you didn't come back.'

In his precise and simple way Chandu had asked me the most fundamental of questions. I should have answered him, there and then. I should have offered him the truth. Instead, I cursed myself. For despite all the emotion, the policeman in me was making a mental note. A note to myself—that I should remember these words, these thoughts that Chandu had spoken.

—

I became a policeman because I crave order and sense in life.

I like things to work out: Money orders delivered by smiling postmen. Trains leaving on time. Tickets for a match or a movie without any fuss. Cheques on the first of each month; tea at four with cinnamon toast; justice for all; happy endings. More than anything else, I prefer a natural and fixed system, a certain sacred law of the group and of the individual.

And because I have spent my entire life tuned into this system, flowing with it, I immediately sense anything that is outside this flow. I don't have to work at it. It just happens. That is why I am a good policeman.

I have worked at this ability, I have polished it. But it was my family and my school and Mussoorie that put me on this course. I can only take credit for honing this skill over time.

My father was a professor, a contented, methodical man, from whom I absorbed love and respect for the systems of both life and nature. And also the ability to live in a world of your own while coping and working with the outside world. From my mother, the most creative housewife you ever saw, I learnt the skill to track shadows disappearing up a faded church wall on a winter evening. She gave me the knowledge that, all things being equal, creating colour-coordinated lunches while humming Gilbert and Sullivan is a vital aspect of life.

With my brother and my sister I discovered the joy and the pain of rivalry, and how to lead a life full of contemplation and commitment, poetry and praise. And my school and Mussoorie gave me the space to test myself, to live. Which was easier, perhaps, than it should have been, because of the friends who gave me much more than I deserved.

Thirty years ago, I left all this behind.

I never wanted to become an IG. It just happened. I was perfectly content to be on my Jawa, solving crimes and mysteries, moving from place to place, going with the flow, always alert to the eddies just above the rapids, the rocks along the shore, and the deep pools under the cliffs. Always on duty, to keep the world moving along with some of the sense and order I so crave.

As I became more and more famous, and took on more and more responsibilities, Mussoorie, in much more than simply the physical sense, remained the vital part of me. Chandu was right. It made me feel very good to tell people I was from Mussoorie.

But why hadn't I come back for all these years?

As I've said, there's no easy answer. Perhaps I didn't want to break the flow—the flow that kept me going, and guided me to solutions and answers. I needed to stay taut, alive to the flow. Coming back to Mussoorie would have meant breaking that flow, giving in to the senses. Mussoorie was like a womb, and I think I feared its promise of comfort—if I returned to it, I might not want to go back and face the world.

And now here I was, back in Mussoorie, overcome with emotion and yet making mental notes—policeman's notes—about a man who was the true source of all that Mussoorie meant to me.

4

I FINALLY ANSWERED Chandu with a half-truth of my own. A half-truth that revealed much more than it concealed.

'Chandu, what can I say? Why didn't I come back? The truth is, I actually never left. That's what my uncle told once me. He said that no matter where I go, I will never really leave Mussoorie.'

'He was right, Allan-baba. Just like a truly great film never really leaves a cinema hall, or our hearts.'

The mention of films made me turn to him with a question, but I checked myself. This wasn't the time for it. But Chandu had a question, and he said it softly.

'Sahib, why didn't you ever get married? By this time you should have been a grandfather.'

'Forget about me, Chandu. Why didn't you ever get married? There wasn't a girl in Mussoorie—from Landour to Library—who wasn't crazy about you. All the tourist-heroes sitting on the railings along the Mall were zeroes compared to you.'

He chuckled again. 'You exaggerate, sahib. I was just a poor, uneducated pahari who checked tickets at Rialto.'

'That you were. But you also kicked a football harder than Ajay Mark, and could run faster than even Champa. And from certain angles, people said you looked like a young Dilip Kumar!'

'Now, sahib, that is too much!'

'And you had the biggest heart in all of Mussoorie. Ask this little schoolboy, whom you showed dozens of films, free of charge, and fed so many aloo-tikkis and Cokes and ice creams. And whom you treated not as a ten-year-old kid, but a trusted friend.'

That was too much emotion for reticent Chandu, and he suddenly said, 'Sahib, Salim, the chai-wala, he's still there!'

'I don't believe it!'

'But the peanut-wala in Landour Bazaar passed away. And Vital Stores closed down.'

'And Rialto almost did, too. Forever.'

Chandu looked away, and then back.

'Sahib, where has that Paul gone to? How you two used to come sprinting down the Kulri slope! Slipping like little goldfish through the crowds of tourists, racing to see who would be the first to reach the Rialto gate!'

'Paul is still a badmash—but he's doing some good work in life, I gather. I've almost lost touch with him. I must find his number and call him, now that I'm back.'

'You and he wouldn't miss any Saturday morning show.'

The mists shifted briefly and the early sun lit a patch of hill behind him. And I asked him the question.

'Chandu, this *tamasha* last night at Rialto—Khanna-sahib told me all about it on the phone. But I forgot to ask him—what was the film showing last night?'

I had to ask this question. I had no choice. It had come in the flow. Something in the collective scrapbook of my senses had been touched.

Chandu answered without a pause, 'Arre, sahib— what difference does it make? The lady has disappeared, and still hasn't been found.'

'Chandu,' I said with an intensity that surprised even me, 'the lady will be found. I'm sure of that. But what was the film last night?'

Chandu looked straight at me, as if seeing me for the first time as a fifty-year-old policeman instead of a ten-year-old kid. Then those eyes, even the bad one, crinkled into the sweetest of smiles. 'Now I understand, sahib, why you are such a great policeman. You should see your own eyes right now. They are totally focused on only the truth, and will not rest until they find it.'

Shamed by his gentleness, I apologized. 'I'm sorry, Chandu, to be like this. We meet after thirty years, here, at my most favourite place in the whole world, and I behave like a policeman with you. With you! The only real hero in my life.'

Without a word, Chandu turned away from me. I thought I had either confused him, or made him cry. But then I heard him singing, almost to himself. I knew the words he was singing even before I heard them or understood them.

'Zindabad, zindabad
Aei mohabbat, zindabad!'

As Chandu repeated the opening line, he turned back to me, and I joined in, out of tune as usual, but his deep, rich voice embracing and forgiving mine.

Together, with an understanding as natural as that between a stream and a river, we both sang out through the mists to the facing hill, on top of which the Haunted House sat like an ancient and favourite aunt at Christmas. The mists smothered both the aunt and the echo of our voices, so we sang in even richer and deeper tones, standing tall and proud, my arm around Chandu's shoulders, until, finally, the echo conquered the mists, and we, in awe, were hushed into silence at the memory of the great Rafi himself.

I would have gladly stood there for eternity, with

the warmth of Chandu a comforting tomb, our memories scattered petals, and the immortal voice of Rafi our *kafan*.

—

So the film last night at Rialto had been a rerun of *Mughal-e-Azam*. And I had chosen that night of all nights to call Khanna in Mussoorie from the crossroads at Chhuttmalpur. That night of all nights to return to my hometown, to risk the taut logic of my wearying life, desperate for a balm, though I feared it might break the flow forever.

Mughal-e-Azam is Chandu's all-time favourite film. He had shown it to us—free of charge, of course— every Saturday afternoon that it ran at Rialto when it released in Mussoorie in 1960. Paul and I were about ten, and Chandu nineteen. He would insist that we see the film after our English morning matinee, and would explain in passionate, if brief, detail every mood and moment, every subtle nuance, of Saleem and Anarkali's romance.

Paul and I, in spite of our scepticism about Hindi films, fell under the spell of both *Mughal-e-Azam* and Chandu's passion for it. In the intimate darkness of Rialto, Dilip Kumar was not only larger than life, he was life itself. And Madhubala, for our ten-year-old hearts and bodies, was all the magic and mystery of desire. So much so, that on the second viewing, smuggled into a box-seat by Chandu, Paul and I joined in on '*Zindabad, zindabad*' as if all the weight and woes of love had descended only on the two of us that day.

This was when I realized that upon growing up, I wanted to be like either Saleem or Chandu—with Chandu being the winner by a nose, since he was actual flesh and blood, and waiting outside Rialto with aloo-tikkis and Cokes for us.

For the rest of my life, Chandu remained my hero. And whenever and wherever I came across *Mughal-e-Azam*—even if the cinema hall had none of the magic of Rialto—I would watch the film with the same wonder. Over the years I aged, at least physically, but Saleem and Chandu never did. Not in the world of my dreams.

5

'Sahib, I knew that *Mughal-e-Azam* would make you emotional again, and I wasn't sure if you would be comfortable. That is why I hesitated to tell you the name of last night's film.'

By this time we had managed to compose ourselves, and the magic of Rafi's memory had slipped away into the mists.

'I understand, Chandu, I understand. But I am glad we sang together, I have done too many things all by myself for so many years.'

Nothing more could be said—further words would be useless, like a clanging bucket coming up from a deep, dry well.

The mists had begun to lift, and in the weak sunlight the path up from my uncle's bench to the old family house beckoned gently. The house where none of my family lived anymore. My parents had passed away, and the rest of the family—beloved aunts and uncles and cousins included—were now scattered all over the world, returning home for the now all too infrequent Christmas get-togethers. Or so I gathered from the lengthy, emotional letters that found me each time, even when I was as far from home as life could take me.

We turned from the bench, I leading the way because the path was too narrow for us to walk side by side—and because Chandu let me.

It was only another fifty yards to the ancient and collapsing wooden gate leading to the back of the house, and as we creaked through, the chowkidar's dog began barking and a voice called out of the awakening morning to silence it. I was a stranger, and yet welcome.

It was too early for even cricket to have started on the tennis court, but I stopped by the so often mended fence, to think of old times. And then we were off, Chandu and I.

We walked along the Eyebrow path which edges towards town across the face of the mountain, past solitary bungalows where mortals and ghosts of memsahibs sleep side by side, past the beginnings of little childhood *pagdandis* which now fade away before the first bend, past the still amazing view to the south where the Mussoorie rampart bows at the feet of the Doon Valley, past the rock where my grandfather used to sit and ruminate, past my old school, past the playground where my brother and I discovered the joys of competition.

And throughout the long walk, as an unhurried and intimate commentary leads you through the best of Test matches, Chandu filled me in on the night before at Rialto, and the history of Mussoorie in the years that I was away. We stopped just once, at Omi's in Landour Bazaar, to pound on the closed shutters and demand tea and samosas in the name of youthful friendships.

'Would you believe it, sahib, that lady's husband fell asleep while watching *Mughal-e-Azam*! At the interval they didn't even come out for a cup of tea.'

'I don't believe you, Chandu—Madhubala and Dilip Kumar in Mussoorie and he falls asleep?'

'People live strange lives, sahib.'

A solitary and ancient coolie drifted past us, looking for early-morning work, even as the first truck groaned up from the Clock Tower.

'Sahib, the traffic through here is unbelievable now—traffic jams right here in Landour! So much has changed.'

'At least good old Rialto is back in business.'

'Yes, sahib. Mussoorie without Rialto—it was unimaginable.'

A group of young cricketers, headed for Survey

Field, came laughing by, pads slung over shoulders, bats in hand. I almost asked them to sprint with me to the field, so that I could face a few overs. Instead, I imagined them returning in the afternoon, sweaty and happy after a morning well spent, and said to Chandu, 'Why can't I be fourteen again, Chandu?'

He smiled and said nothing, and we walked on, past silent shops that met all the mundane requirements of a hill-station life, and the still sleepy Post Office. We passed the corner where the peanut-wala used to hunch over his little fire, then crossed under the Clock Tower, where time has truly stood still—though wise Ruskin Bond claims that it happens only in Shamli.

Thukral's photography shop, below the Clock Tower, hadn't opened yet, the shutters down to guard its treasure chest of fading black and white moments. Next to it used to be Picture Palace, Rialto's only true rival, but it had closed down forever.

Chandu and I stood there awhile, agreeing how sad this was, and then I was pleasantly surprised to see my old friend Anil—out on a jog that was, in fact, a brisk walk at best—approach us, waving his arms. After a big hug and a laugh, he said he was doing this on strict doctor's orders, to compensate for years of excess. Then we were off with Anil to Brentwood Hotel for a round of tea.

Inevitably, the mysterious disappearance of the lady at Rialto came up.

Anil asked me what I made of it all and I replied that I knew too little to make anything of it yet. 'All I know is that the man wasn't a film buff—he fell asleep watching *Mughal-e-Azam*!'

'He did, sahib. I had to go and wake him up when the film ended. He was snoring like a steam engine. And when he discovered that his wife was missing, he immediately ordered me to begin searching for her.'

We were joined at Brentwood by Sunny (Anil's 'partner in prime'), who gave us his own take on what really happened at Rialto, which was not very different from Anil's opinion. And then the conversation drifted to old school friends and long-ago cricket matches on Survey Field. When Chandu and I finally moved reluctantly on, it was already well past 8 a.m., the time I'd arranged to meet Khanna at Rialto.

Outside, Chandu said, 'Sahib, I don't want to disagree with what Anil-sahib and Sunny-sahib said, but I am sure that the husband had nothing to do with the lady's disappearance. Yes, he was complaining a lot about watching a movie on such a cold night in Mussoorie, but he calmed down when his wife said he should do it just for her.'

We walked back from Brentwood, up the path to the top of Kulri hill—the short cut Paul and I often took to avoid the gabble of tourists on the Mall. At Windy Corner, in front of Fashion Fabrics, I suddenly felt the cold. There was a hint of snow in the air.

'The police searched everywhere for her. Khanna-sahib spared no effort, even though it was the middle of the night. Policemen searched on foot all around Rialto, and then in every corner of Mussoorie. Jeeps went all the way to Kempti, all the way to the Toll Gate at Kolhukhet, all the way along Tehri Road to Seokholi. But no sign of her.'

Rialto was only minutes away, but I lingered a while at Windy Corner, watching the valley tremble faintly in the weak sunlight, wanting to prolong the rediscovery of my hometown in the company of an old friend who had kept all my best memories alive and safe.

Chandu stood beside me, squinting into the distance. When the sun finally broke out over the valley and I turned to resume our walk, he said, 'So why are you still alone, sahib? Last time you avoided my question. Why haven't you married? Is it because you never found the woman of your dreams?'

In reply I just nodded my head, took him by the arm and we jogged down towards Rialto, past a whole row of shuttered shops that used to be a silent, mossy wall when Paul and I would get into our final dash for the matinee on Saturday mornings.

—

Yes, it is because I never found the woman of my dreams.

Or maybe it is because I have too many dreams. Impossible dreams.

In my dreams, women are so beautiful, so mysterious, so desirable, that I can never believe they would actually be interested in me.

In the few relationships where we have managed to come close, the women grow weary of my awe, and ask instead for love. Of which I have none to give.

6

I NOTICED THAT Chandu had drifted away slightly as we crossed under Kwality and made our way to the outer gate of Rialto and through the tunnel-like, poster-lined entry way. I entered the square in front of Hamers, and the actual cinema hall, to the smell of frying aloo-tikkis, and saw Khanna—with two other police officers I did not know—Arora-sahib, the manager of Rialto, and Jot Singh, the chairman of the City Board, rise from their chairs to greet me. There was a well-dressed, prosperous-looking man already on his feet and pacing. Clearly the businessman-husband.

I went up to the men. Chandu stood back, and I realized that he had drifted away not from me, but back to his rightful place in the society governed by the gentlemen rising from their chairs—a ticket-checker's place was not among them.

What followed was a cacophony of greetings and good-natured abuse, broken repeatedly by the deep voice of the missing lady's husband as he pointed to his shiny gold watch which he swore was now registering 9.15, when I had promised to be there by eight. How could the great Allan Kohli be so irresponsible when a man's wife was missing?

I apologized, because there was no way I could have made him understand that through all my emotional wanderings, for the past eight hours or so, ever since that telephone call to Khanna at the thana, one part of me had been thinking only of his missing wife.

He took my apology surprisingly well, and this made me stop for a moment and reassess him. He was more than the sum of his gold watch, his pomposity, the complaining voice and the Ikon, complete with uniformed driver, that I had seen parked under Kwality. There were faint laugh lines in the excessive flesh around his eyes, and there was a hint of dignity in his bearing.

Having accepted my apology, he sat down with the rest of us and we began a serious appraisal of the situation. Even Arora-sahib swallowed the last of his latest line of jokes along with a swig of tea. One of Khanna's men presented me with a very thorough file on the night's events. It began with eyewitness reports of those who had actually been at Rialto (it turned out that precisely nine other people were watching the show, all of whom had been contacted in the middle of the night), and then gave a detailed account of the search operations conducted through the night. There was a fairly good description of what the lady was wearing, and what she looked like ('Black *salwar kameez*, dark grey shawl, slightly high-heeled black shoes, small black purse. Lady small in stature, greying hair, middle or late fifties'). The husband did not have a picture of his wife with him, nor could he confirm her exact age, according to the report.

As I glanced through the pages, I felt the eyes of the husband upon me, even as steaming hot tea and aloo-tikkis arrived for everyone. I was happily informed that the tikkis had been made by the son of the man who produced the same wonders thirty years ago. I took a sip and a bite, and looked up at the husband for another assessment.

The wrong side of sixty (or maybe the right side—who knows!), he was short and wide, but not unattractive. The look of concern on his face was sincere, if not truly touching.

Without hesitation, I told him that I would find his wife within forty-eight hours.

He nodded, and sat back in his chair, refusing the aloo-tikkis. He was a businessman, and he knew I was talking business.

I had noticed in the report that we had his mobile

number and his Delhi home number. Contacting him would not be a problem. So, without further ado, I said, 'Sir, I think the best thing for you to do would be to return to Delhi. Leave things here in my hands. I will be speaking to you within forty-eight hours, if not sooner. If we have any further questions to ask you, we'll get in touch.'

He immediately rose to his feet, shook my hand, thanked me, saying that it was only because I was handling the case that he was returning to Delhi, and then shook Khanna's hand without any thanks. Whereupon he strode, with some vigour for a man of his size and age, out through the entry tunnel of Rialto, shouting for his driver, oblivious to the posters of Madhubala—and Aishwarya Rai and Demi Moore— urging him to stay.

As soon as he was gone, the cacophony started up again, and the crowd in the square grew as the news spread that I was back. It took all of my vanishing self-control to put an end to the remembrances and the jokes and the tall tales which sprung up like brilliant character-actors stealing the thunder from a slightly ponderous hero. It could have gone on for longer than the thirty years I had been gone, and I would have enjoyed every minute of it.

But the first rush of emotions at my homecoming behind me, my instincts were awake and sharp again. I asked Khanna, even as he was thanking me for the third time for getting rid of the husband, who had actually seen the wife.

The same officer who had presented me with the file promptly answered, 'Chandu, Salim, the chai-wala, Bhola, the ticket seller, and five out of the nine people watching the show. No one else saw her.'

Before I could congratulate the officer on both his report and his prompt reply, Arora-sahib, with a great guffaw, quipped. 'I don't think the husband has ever actually seen the wife either!'

Khanna, trying not to laugh too hard, said that the officer who had presented the file was from Kumaon, and not Garhwal, and that was why he was so sharp. This prompted a whole series of comments and jibes, mainly starting and ending with Jot Singh, until the other officer present, a Garhwali, sobered us down by explaining that with the creation of Uttaranchal we were all one. This discussion could have taken us on another long and merry journey, but a slightly more serious Khanna brought us back to the matter at hand.

'Allan, I didn't want to say this in front of the husband, but almost everyone who saw the wife commented on how beautiful she is.'

Which brought Arora-sahib back into his element. 'How lucky some of us are, to have younger and beautiful wives!' he roared. 'And mine is still with me!'

—

I used to play badminton with Arora-sahib's wife, all of those thirty years ago, and she was definitely younger and more beautiful than her husband. Which, of course, led to great ribaldry, but never even a hint of jealousy from Arora-sahib. In fact, the two of them seemed to share that rarest of marital relationships in which friendship dominates.

Mrs Arora and I never did manage to win the Mussoorie mixed doubles title, but we came close. To winning, that is.

7

THE PERSON I most wanted to talk with now was Bhandari-*kaka*, the projectionist at Rialto for the past forty-five faithful years, and who, Arora-sahib informed me, was still going strong.

But I would save Kaka for the last.

For the time being, I let myself drift, the conversations flowing lazily around me like warm air from a winter fire. And it finally dawned on me that I was back in Mussoorie, and at peace.

I wasn't just back in Mussoorie—but back in Mussoorie on a case. Mussoorie and a case. Silk and steel. Deep pools and sudden rapids. Memories and the moment. Prithviraj Kapoor and Dilip Kumar. Tea and tandoori chicken. Rajesh Khanna and Amitabh Bachchan. The Beatles and the Rolling Stones.

I felt someone's gaze upon me, and I turned to find Chandu looking at me, a cup of steaming tea in his hands, right eye squinted over the cup.

I asked where I could find Salim, the chai-wala, and Arora-sahib, with yet another guffaw, replied, 'With Anarkali!'

Jot Singh clarified, 'Don't you remember? Salim's only true love is Anarkali, his tea-kettle. You'll find them together right now, in the canteen.'

I excused myself, saying I might be gone a while, so if people wanted to meet me later, that would be fine. Khanna invited me home for lunch and insisted I should then stay on with him. The policeman from Kumaon wanted to accompany me, and that felt right to me, so the two of us walked together into the musty embrace of Rialto.

Little had changed, except for the price of the tickets. The magic, even on an off-season winter morning, was still strong. The half-darkness, the sense of grit and glamour, the feeling of time moving at a different pace—and then the four entry doors, with their curtains at half-mast, like temple gates at the four *dhams* during the winter months.

If a young Chandu had come striding up to me, smile on his lips and understanding in his eyes and free tickets in his hand, I would not have been surprised.

But it was Salim who appeared instead, right where I had last seen him thirty years ago, scrubbing down Anarkali with a mixture of charcoal and hot water.

It looked like Salim could do with some scrubbing

too. He saw me, and a wide smile opened up his grimy face.

'*Huzoor*, huzoor—what a pleasure! A great man like you has come to grace our humble cinema hall!'

Salim, too, had not changed.

'Salim-sahib, when I drank the tea offered to us outside, I knew by its taste and quality that it could not have been made by you. So I've come to sample the true taste of tea that only your Anarkali can produce.'

Salim's smile widened, and we were now on even terms.

Salim and Chandu, probably because of spending day after day after day in such close proximity, had become much like Mohan Bagan and East Bengal with their little running battles, revolving mainly around the general cleanliness of Salim's canteen, and the quality of his tea. But, inspite of this, the two of them were known to have a peg or two together if the mood was mellow, or if the right film was running at Rialto.

As Salim prepared the tea, with all the loving care of a true housewife, I asked him if he had noticed anything special last night.

This led to a long, rambling description of the husband ('that lala with a big mouth and a small heart'), the wife ('beautiful beyond words'), the interval (no tea was ordered by the two, even though Salim had made an *elaichi*-brew in anticipation), the post-show drama ('he tried to treat Chandu and me like his servants, ordering us to search for his wife—even in the ladies' toilet!'), and the outstanding role of Bhandari-kaka in handling the whole situation. Apparently Kaka had led them all in a search of the area around Rialto, and then convinced the husband to go to the police station in his car—after checking with the driver and the local STD-wala as to whether they had seen the wife ('Of course the lala only took Kaka in the car, Chandu and I had to walk!').

'And then, huzoor, I was right there with Chandu when you called Khanna-sahib from Chhuttmalpur. It was as if you were a prophet sent from heaven. The entire mood of the group immediately changed. When that lala heard that you were coming—the great IG Allan Kohli—he stopped shouting about how he was going to call the *Pradhan Mantriji*.'

This brought a chuckle in affirmation from the Kumaoni.

'And, huzoor, the person most happy to hear that you were returning was Chandu. Even his one good eye was sparkling!'

The tea had arrived, and we two policemen sat back and relished it, for it was really good.

Seeing us enjoying his tea, Salim was silent for a while, only nodding in response to our '*wah, wahs*'.

Then he requested me to step outside, behind Arora-sahib's office.

Which I did, and the Kumaoni understood.

'Huzoor, this is for your ears only.'

I could sense that this was the moment of a lifetime for Salim. He had been an 'extra' all his life, and now, finally, he had a 'speaking part'.

I gave him my full concentration.

'Huzoor, something different did happen last night! Now you know that Chandu never, ever orders tea from me. At least for the past forty years he hasn't. But last night he did. One cup. Special. Lots of sugar. Nice and hot.'

Salim glanced around, to make sure that Chandu was not in sight. He wasn't.

I asked, 'Did Chandu drink it himself?'

'I don't know, huzoor. He ordered it for the interval, took it, even paid for it!—then walked off, without any comment, towards the main entrance, where the ticket window and the stairs up to the projection room are. After that I fell asleep, because it was cold and it had been a long day. I fell asleep wondering about Chandu and his tea. I vaguely remember hearing a song in the second half, and didn't fully wake up till the lala began shouting that he would call the Pradhan Mantriji if his wife wasn't found!'

—

I notice that tea has dominated the narration of my

walk through Mussoorie—besides the case of the missing lady, of course. Tea at Omi's with Chandu, tea at Brentwood with Anil and Sunny, tea in front of Rialto with the whole gang, and that very special tea of Salim and Anarkali's with the Kumaoni policeman.

Tea is not quite an addiction (my aunt always quotes a Chinese proverb which states that the seventh cup opens the door to heaven), but on cold winter mornings in the hills, tea is the best blanket in the world. It wraps itself around your stomach and your heart, just as you wrap your hands around the steaming cup, or, better still, the glass.

8

WHEN SALIM AND I returned to the canteen, the Kumaoni policeman (I finally had to ask him his name again—I'm hopeless with names; he said it was Veer) was talking to a youngish, shy-looking man who turned out to be Bhola, the ticket seller.

Since Veer and Bhola were already in conversation, I sat down and listened.

It appeared that Bhola could not be contacted last night after the show, so Veer was questioning him now. Bhola said that after selling the final two tickets to the husband and wife, he did his *hisaab* ('only eleven tickets were sold, so it wasn't too difficult'), went to Neelams for dinner since he had just received his pay, and then—here he became even more shy—went to see his lady-love at Library Bazaar. Which was why Veer couldn't find him last night, because the lady-love had to be met in secret.

Veer was very good with the young man, not

prying into his love life, and simply acknowledging it with a nod.

When asked how long he had been working at Rialto, Bhola answered that Chandu had got him the job just two years ago, because he was from Chandu's village, just across the Aglar river.

Then Veer asked, 'Tell us about the husband and wife. Did you notice anything special or different about them?'

'Well, sahib, I had almost closed the counter when the two of them arrived. She came up to the window, and he stood back, complaining about the cold and how tired he was. But she just turned and smiled at him, and asked him to please do this just for her sake. That silenced him for a while, but after she bought the tickets, and the two of them walked away inside, I heard his complaining start up again.'

'And the woman? What was she like?'

Here Bhola hesitated for a moment, his head at an angle, as if to find the right words for his thoughts. That was when I saw a young Chandu in Bhola.

'Sahib, she reminded me of one of those heroines from the old movies. You know, the ones who worked with Guru Dutt and Raj Kapoor. From the black-and-white films. Especially since she was wearing black, and the light outside was so shadowy.'

Veer had been noting down everything Bhola was

saying, but this description stopped him.

It stopped me, too. Stopped me from pondering over how romance forty years ago must have been so different from romance today. Stopped me from thinking of the black-and-white heroines of my own dreams. Stopped me from drifting away again into the mists and memories of my mind and Mussoorie.

Bhola's words should have done just the opposite. But they didn't. That is the curse of being a policeman.

I was well and truly back on a case again.

—

I was struck by how much Bhola reminded me of Chandu, especially by what he'd said about those old films and their heroines.

As I have said earlier, Chandu, at the time of *Mughal-e-Azam*'s release, was, for a ten-year-old me, about as romantic as a man could be. Not a romantic in the limited sense of just appealing to the ladies, and vice versa, but a man who lived his life in a romantic way.

The way he stood, as if fully aware of the world, and yet in a world of his own.

The way he spoke, choosing his words carefully when required, and launching into the fullest of emotions, though still in control, when the mood was right. The way he treated others, with love and respect, and yet polite aloofness when they disturbed him.

The way he played football, with ease in the effort. The way he held a *bidi*, or a glass of tea, as if they were companions on life's voyage. The way he knew his place, and yet was proud. The way he treated two ten-year-olds as equals, and yet with wisdom.

9

BHANDARI-KAKA WAS NOT due at Rialto until around 2 p.m. (there was no morning show), so I decided to walk with Veer to the thana. I half expected Chandu to join us, but he simply waved to us from the tea shop as we walked by.

Crossing through the entry way, suddenly hemmed in by film posters, I asked Veer which his favourite movies were.

'Sir, where do I find time for films? But haan, I really liked *Sarfarosh*. Aamir made a first-class cop. The others in his group were really good, too. Very natural. And the Muslim cop was excellent. Now I want to see *Lagaan*, but I missed it on its first round at Rialto. It will be back soon, so I'll catch it then.'

We walked on for a while in silence, and I knew that he wanted to ask me something, when suddenly the youthful Bhola arrived bounding at our side. I turned just in time to catch his last strides. He ran well, like Chandu used to.

'Sahib, sahib—I must talk to you. Just for a moment.'

It appeared to be heading for another scene like the one with Salim, and I didn't want to insult Veer by asking him to move on. But Veer understood, and Bhola and I stood in front of Cambridge Book Depot as the shutters were being raised and Bhola told me what he wanted to tell me.

I listened intently, and my senses shivered to attention. Bhola's words, Veer's back disappearing down the slope below the Railway Out-Agency, the Cambridge Book Depot's shutters reaching their peak—everything was in slow-motion harmony, as the purest excitement blossomed within me, like a prelude to the best of sex—both a beginning and an end.

Then the universe returned to its natural speed again. I thanked Bhola, told him not to worry (also told him to give my love to his lady), and shouted out to Veer to wait, even as Mr Arora, the owner of Cambridge Book Depot, recognized me and called out that copies of my cousin's latest book had come in.

I thanked him too, and, as I jogged off in pursuit of Veer, promised to be back to buy a copy.

I caught up with Veer above Anil's house. He had one foot up on the railing, looking out to the Doon Valley—in the manner of his favourite actor, Aamir

Khan, but I think the pose was unintentional.

'Veer, you wanted to ask me something?'

Again that sincere nod.

'Yes, sir, but not about the case directly.'

'Those are the most interesting questions, Veer.'

'Right, sir. I just wanted to ask which your favourite films are.'

How could I answer that one? By saying that Dilip Kumar and Madhubala share my humble bachelor lodgings? By saying that Rajesh Khanna and Sharmila Tagore still sing together in my dreams?

Instead, I said, 'Basically, I gave up on Hindi films some time ago. But I will see *Sarfarosh*. And maybe we can watch *Lagaan* together. I think I might enjoy them both.'

—

What was the magic of Hindi films? What is the magic?

When I was ten, and Chandu showed us *Mughal-e-Azam*, and explained to our almost innocent hearts the wonder of the romance, I could actually feel it all, there, in the 'close and holy darkness', surrounded by people and yet totally alone.

Nine years later, when I took my first love (or infatuation) to see the same film, I was torn between the reality of her and the fantasy on screen, and that was the magic, especially when she touched my hand in the dark and reality and fantasy briefly came together.

At about the same time, Rajesh and Sharmila swept into my dreams, and to watch them sing together was so intimate, so perfect, that I had to experience their films alone.

Then one day I saw a film that had no Rajesh, no Sharmila, no intimate perfection, only violence and corruption, and the magic was lost.

Sounds too pat, I suppose, but that, at least, is how it was for me. This is my story, the only one I can truly tell.

Since then, it has been reruns of *Mughal-e-Azam* on screen, and of *Aradhana* and *Amar Prem* on TV.

I might just give *Sarfarosh* a shot, though.

10

I WAS BECOMING increasingly impressed with Veer. Over
lunch at Khanna's house, he partook lightly of the rich
Punjabi repast which Mrs Khanna spread out before us
(the Khannas partook rather less lightly), and he handled
her sensual teasing with an equally light touch. He
refused to call her Bhabhiji—which I did, with great
indulgence—and kept referring to her as Madam even
after she forbade him to do so. 'Such formal behaviour
will get you nowhere,' she admonished him, and added,
'and it won't get *me* anywhere either,' which he
pretended not to hear.

What impressed me most of all was that every now
and then he would, almost casually, ask those oblique
questions which can reveal so little and gain so much.

And one of these questions, slipped neatly in
between Mrs Khanna's fourth forceful offering of
mutter-paneer and Veer's polite refusal, brought an
interesting response. Veer had asked Mrs Khanna when

she had last seen *Mughal-e-Azam*, and her reply was that she would love to see the film again, but Khanna never took her to the movies anymore and that he would lose her one day on account of this. This prompted Khanna to promise her that he would take her to the movies soon. And then he added that walking past Rialto last night between 11 and 11.30, he had been stopped in his tracks by the song '*Zindabad, zindabad*' coming from Rialto much louder than usual. The song had made him feel nostalgic, and very romantic—whereupon (this was said with a delightful wink) he had rushed home to his loving wife.

Hearing this, Mrs Khanna then winked at me, and said, in that melting voice of hers, 'What did I tell you, Allan, when you called last night? That lalaji from Delhi disturbed your friend just when things were getting interesting? Now you have proof!'

She leaned forward to say this, and, just for emphasis, her silk dupatta slipped down her bosom like the clouds slipping off the snow peaks that you see from Lal Tibba.

Veer blushed, in a very manly fashion. And Khanna suppressed a smile, thoroughly enjoying himself.

Bhabhiji was outdoing herself that afternoon. And much though I hated to walk away from the performance, I excused myself and hurried off to meet Bhandari-kaka, before he got busy with the three o'clock show.

Things were now moving in a flow that almost left me breathless—

But, once again, tea was to interrupt.

As I bounded down the stairs from Khanna's house—perched on the slope like one of Bhabhiji's samosas on a tilted tea tray—to the Mall Road, I was met by Rawat, the ancient policeman who had been serving on the Mussoorie force for what seemed like centuries. His main job was the providing of hot tea and gossip to the entire thana at all hours of the day and night.

He could see that I was in a hurry—but I could see that he wanted to talk with me, so I greeted him warmly. Besides, he had probably served tea to my grandfather in his day.

'Allan-sahib, I will not delay you with pointless chatter like our dear Mrs Khanna. I know that you have promised that lalaji to find his wife within forty-eight hours. All of Mussoorie knows this, and all of Mussoorie also knows that you will do exactly that. It is in this connection that I must speak to you. If you wish, we can walk together and I will tell you my story along the way.'

The pace of Rawat's walk along the Mall is notoriously leisurely—and everyone in Mussoorie knows this—but I could think of nothing to defer him, so off we went. Schoolboys and tourists and Tibetans and the odd missionary passed us—as, almost, did the afternoon itself.

'Allan-sahib, when everyone collected at the thana last night after the show, I, naturally, had to make tea. But even before I could finish making the tea, Veer-sahib took lalaji off to Khanna-sahib's house. Meanwhile, Chandu and Salim showed up on foot, so I gave them the tea instead, even though Salim has never liked my tea.'

We were nearing Hakmans by this time, and I remembered watching Jagte Raho at the Capitol Cinema there during the blackout of the 1971 war. That had been my last visit to Mussoorie. The way Rawat was talking and walking, it was not sheer chance that I remembered *Jagte Raho*.

'Allan-sahib, now I will get to the point. I too am a policeman, so I too notice things. And now I will tell you what I noticed.'

Time had almost stood still once again, even though we were a good distance from the Clock Tower.

'Chandu was very keen to go to Khanna's house to find out the latest on the search. So he and I set off on foot, leaving Salim to sip my tea at the thana. Now, sahib, I used to be able to see in the dark. I could walk from Jabbarkhet to Library on a moonless night, without a torch, taking all the short cuts, and never stumble, even on the steepest slopes. But now, sahib, the years have taken their toll.'

We were almost back at Cambridge Book Depot, and I was very keen to buy my cousin's latest book. But Rawat and his tale, like the Pied Piper and his pipe, took me straight on to the Rialto entry way—

'So, Allan-sahib, as we made our way to Khanna-sahib's house, I asked Chandu to use his torch. And he said he had left it at Rialto! Can you believe that, Allan-sahib? Chandu leaving his torch behind? His one and only torch, which he keeps with him day and night! That old, trustworthy torch which he has had for at least forty years! The torch with which he has checked lakhs of tickets! The torch that is more dear to him than anything else in the world! He left it behind at Rialto! Allan-sahib, can you believe that?'

I'm afraid I could not express my belief or disbelief, or even hear the complete description of the torch, for I was already running up the Kulri slope from Kwality, past Bamboo's brothers' pork shop, then under Art Press, under the Tavern, and off towards Landour and the Eyebrow and my grandfather's rock.

Bhandari-kaka would be at Rialto for the rest of the day and into the night. Right then I needed to run and run and run until I reached the one place where I needed to be at the moment to still the strange restlessness inside me.

And turning in front of the memory that Picture

Palace now was, steeling myself for the climb up towards the Clock Tower and Landour Bazaar, I felt Chandu's gaze upon me, like a blessing, as he leaned on the gate of Union Church, smoking a bidi as if it were a beloved companion on life's voyage.

—

I have tried to explain, somewhat unsuccessfully, the magic of Hindi films.

And the magic of running?

Running up the slope to the Clock Tower, my legs were already beginning to ache across the thighs, my lungs beginning to burn, and my face, as usual, beginning to turn red with the strain and the effort— and my grandfather's rock was still a tough three kilometres away.

So why was I running? I have no one, complete answer, only parts of the puzzle—I was fairly good with puzzles in school.

Nothing, to me, tests your endurance like a race or long-distance running. Overcoming the strain and the effort brings a tremendous feeling of satisfaction when the race is over, or the destination has been reached. It also keeps you looking good for the ladies of your dreams.

But the deepest truth is that running, like so few other things in our messy, imperfect world, is still pure and simple. It is you, your body—your being—and a challenge.

And in the purity and simplicity of running, the mind and soul are cleansed—at least for a few moments—of that stubborn restlessness, that weariness, the kind that had driven me out of Saharanpur to the crossroads at Chhuttmalpur.

—

11

THE LAST STRETCH up from the school gate to the rock
was a killer. (Paul and I used to make it from Rialto to
the school gate in fourteen minutes—I must have taken
at least twice as long now.) Gasping for breath, I halted
below the rock on the Eyebrow, just where there is the
big bend and the tremendous view of the valley. Hands
on knees, head hanging, chest heaving, I'm afraid I had
no time for the view.

It was at this moment that the magic was
completed—even before I fully caught my breath, before
I climbed up to my grandfather's rock, before the
eagles soaring high out across the valley made their
turn for home and the clock at St George's struck the
hour.

The angle of the breeze must have changed, for it
brought with it, suddenly, music from a radio at the
Suncliff servants' quarters, deep in the forest, two
bends away along the Eyebrow—music faint but true.

And for the third time that day, '*Zindabad, zindabad— aei mohabbat zindabad*' flowed from yesterday into today, bringing with it the scent of memories and mourning, the fast-fading taste of eternal love.

I turned and went sprinting towards Suncliff, my legs young again, the narrow Eyebrow a carpet of welcome for my lengthening strides, even the stones underfoot made way for my true homecoming. Rafi's voice dipped and vanished when I swept back into the folds of the hill, and rose again, in a glorious excess of romantic passion, as I rounded a bend.

When I reached the point above Suncliff where the water pipe used to cut across the path, the song was reaching it's climax. I leaned against the side of the *khud*, closed my eyes, and knew, even as the mystery was solved, that the real challenge had only just begun.

The song ended, and the St George's clock struck the hour. But it was a long time before I stood up to move.

—

It has been said about me that in my entire career I have never told a lie.

Which is not entirely true, for to myself I have told so many lies that we are now old friends. But yes—in my work I have not lied, and that adherence to the truth has kept me taut.

It may sound like a difficult thing to do—never telling a lie—but in fact it is surprisingly easy, and, once you start, a very reassuring habit. Because whenever you are faced with a question, you always have the answer, which is the truth. It is as simple as that.

Until, one morning, you ask yourself, 'What is truth?'

12

MY RETURN TO Landour Bazaar and reality was an easy jog, and many friends who had witnessed my frenzied run earlier stopped and questioned me about it—to which, amidst much jesting, I replied that I was simply trying to find my vanishing youth, and I had to sprint to catch up with it.

Which was not as much of a jest as I made it out to be.

I needed to get to the Landour Community Hospital, where I was born. On my way back from Suncliff, I had decided that I would donate blood at LCH. But before I did this, I needed to speak to the missing lady's husband. I called him from the STD booth at the Tehri bus stand.

And have a cup of tea.

Veer had very neatly provided me with lalaji's numbers, and I tried his mobile first, which, unfortunately, seemed to be permanently busy (perhaps lalaji had finally got through to the PM).

Then I did a little mental calculation, and called Rana at the Cheetal Grand near Khatauli, with the hope that if the husband had stopped in Dehra Dun to complete his business, he could be at Cheetal by now.

And I was right. After cheerfully enduring Rana's jibes about my not visiting him for so long, and one or two reminiscences about Corbett Park in the very old days, I was talking with the husband, and was pleasantly surprised by his answers to my rather personal questions.

Yes, his wife had never accompanied him on any business trip before—not in the almost forty years that they had been married.

Yes, it was she who had insisted that they go to Mussoorie to see the film, but he had already told the Mussoorie police that.

Yes, she had got the black salwar kameez stitched especially for this trip—and also bought the low-heeled shoes and grey shawl. How did he know this? Well, he never took much interest in what his wife wore, but this time she had asked for the driver to take her to Kashmiri Gate to a special tailor who was an expert in making clothes in the traditional style—and she wanted only pure cotton, nothing else. This he knew because he overheard this discussion at the breakfast table when his wife called the tailor, and because the driver complained that the car had gotten scraped in the narrow gullies around Kashmiri Gate while searching for very specific shoe and shawl shops.

And—this the husband added on his own—she rummaged through all her old trunks to find the purse, which was made of some kind of black satin. And she also went and got her hair cut in a style which vaguely looked like something out of the 1950s or '60s. Which was a great pity, for the husband was rather fond of her long, albeit greying, hair.

I almost asked him whether he had ever told her this, but I enquired about her shoe size instead.

This question stumped him, and the best that he could manage was that her feet must be quite small.

Her blood type? How in the world would he know? But yes, he had her doctor's number in Delhi, because the doctor was his also. And if I would just hold on, he would get the number from his wallet.

This took him less than a minute, during which time Rana enquired whether, since lalaji seemed to be friend of mine, he should charge the man for a quite generous lunch? I was about to tell Rana to charge the lunch to the PM's Secretariat when the husband was back on the line with the doctor's number. Before I could thank him, he said, 'You know, Kohli-sahib, we really had a good time together on the trip to Dehra Dun. We took a coupe on the Mussoorie Express, at her suggestion, and had the driver bring the car to

Dehra Dun on his own. She has always been a good wife to me, but on this trip she seemed unusually happy. Or, rather, content.'

Then, accepting my reassurances that his wife would be found, lalaji was off to Delhi.

I dialled the doctor's number. The doctor remembered the lady well. 'He is an old patient of mine, and a good one,' he said of the lalaji. And of his wife he said, 'So polite, and so beautiful even at her age. I hope nothing unfortunate has happened to her.'

—

Is there any reason why women age so much more gracefully than men?

I remember once seeing Waheeda Rehman at the Delhi airport, about five years ago. She walked into the departure lounge, by herself, and quietly stood in a corner. Like a field of winter wheat bending in the breeze, the eyes of all the men around turned towards her, one by one.

Aware of the eyes, and yet untroubled by them, she just stood there, totally at ease with her beauty. And because of that ease, there was no lust in any of the eyes—simply admiration, and memories, and gratitude.

13

DONATING BLOOD AT Landour Community Hospital—
known locally as LCH—was a bit more complicated
than I had anticipated, because one of the nurses, who
had been around since I was a child, decided to haul
out my bulky medical file, just for fun, and show it off
to the more recent nurses. It was a novelty, she said
with a laugh when I protested, for the hospital was
now serving the poorer people of the hills instead of
the sahibs and memsahibs and their babas of yesteryears.

But eventually, after great gaiety, and a visit to the
room where the nurse was sure I was born (with an
overcast sky outside, and the afternoon turning into
evening, the room seemed small and almost sad) the
donation was done.

I kept a small bottle of blood for myself, telling the
doctor that I wanted to have it tested in Dehra Dun the
next morning. When the assembled nurses asked what
it was to be tested for, I said, 'Old age!' and was gone

before they could ask any more details.

This done, I was off, down Mullingar Hill to the Bata shop in Landour Bazaar, and the cloth shop near the Clock Tower, where Chandu caught me with my hands full of bundles.

Not having seen him for some hours, Chandu now appeared to me much more real, of mortal flesh and blood, than the beloved memory of the morning. He was emerging from the infamous 'green-curtain shop' when I ran into him. But he had not imbibed too deeply, for he was still very much in his senses. He stood still before me and looked straight into my eyes.

He was about to ask me something when suddenly Arora-sahib came striding down the road, shouting out upon seeing me, 'Arre, Allan-baba, shopping for your girlfriend? The romantic air of Mussoorie has finally gotten to you, too, huh?'

The arrival of Arora-sahib, full of zest and good humour, was a blessing, for I had found myself and Chandu studying each other with far too much concentration.

'Arora-sahib, girlfriends are a thing of the past! I'm going to follow in your esteemed footsteps and get married! That is, if I can find someone younger and very, very beautiful!'

This I said in a voice far too loud for me, and several heads in the shops turned towards me.

'Wah, Allan, wah! This is the spirit! This is the spirit! And who is the unlucky lady you are aiming to capture, may I ask? I hope she plays good badminton— or, better still, bad goodminton!'

Arora-sahib's voice was even louder than mine, and I could see this conversation turning into quite a happening in Landour Bazaar. Right under the blind, timeless eye of the Clock Tower.

And so it did, with Chandu first a somewhat silent spectator, and then a total non-participant. Out of the corner of my eye, I saw him smile slightly and head back in through the 'green curtain', with another fifteen minutes to spare for the spirits before he had to return to Rialto for the six o'clock show.

—

How easy the games we play with people we love.

Small and effortless lies, which harm no one, and let love survive.

I had played these games before only with myself.

14

I CALLED UP Khanna from Ram Chandar's, and said I would be late for dinner, and that the investigation was going well.

Bhabhiji came on the line, giggling with excitement, saying that she hadn't seen Khanna in such a romantic mood for years, and I was to blame. For this I took full credit, and promised to have a much bigger dinner than I had lunch.

Bhabhiji whispered seductively into the phone, 'Don't be too late. I want Khanna all to myself as soon as possible. Also because—and this is even more important—I have invited a special *saheli* for dinner. Slim and elegant, unlike me, poor thing, but full of passion and life. And still unmarried at forty, only because she has never found the perfect man. And—oh, yes—she loves scruffy beards!'

I stroked the stubble on my chin, thanked and bid farewell to Bhabhiji in a deep and husky voice, bought a torch, and set off into the embrace of the darkening, sensual evening.

—

Like Rawat, I too prided myself on never using a torch in Mussoorie—or at least I did thirty years ago.

But I was on duty—on a case—and I had already learnt that the paths and pagdandis of my childhood were now as unfaithful as Shashikala in those black-and-white movies.

Also, I was venturing forth into hills and valleys that were new to me.

15

I ATE FAR too much for dinner.

Much to Bhabhiji's delight, and the bemused wonder of her saheli, who was indeed slim and elegant, and whose eyes hinted at the passion and life lurking within. She even brushed a bit of snow out of my hair (not my beard!) when I arrived, at around 9:30, bringing a blast of cold air in with me.

I was a bit cold myself, and more than a bit damp from the remains of the snow which had covered much of me, but the chair opposite the saheli was beckoning me to the table, and suddenly I was very, very hungry.

The weather had turned for the worse—or for the better—and Mussoorie was cuddling up for a cold winter's night. Which was one reason why I felt so hungry.

Also, because the food was marvellous, as was the company—Khanna and I relaxing together after decades. And because I had got a great deal of exercise in the course of the past eighteen hours, and the restless excitement inside me had now been replaced by the peace that comes to me when all the loose ends have been neatly tied up.

Also, the saheli kept glancing at me out of the corners of those eyes, and this too, oddly, made me feel hungry.

After dinner, as Bhabhiji and her saheli retired to the other room—to compare notes, perhaps—Khanna and I stayed back at the table over coffee, and I asked him, 'How far did your boys go on foot while carrying out the search last night? I know that the entire area around Rialto was fully covered, but did they go down towards the Aglar? Right down?'

Khanna replied in the negative, and then asked what I had in mind.

Before I could reply, the phone rang.

It was Veer, Khanna told me, saying that he wanted permission to take a small party of men and make one more thorough search in the early morning.

Before I could say anything, Khanna was telling him that it was pointless, especially in the snow. But I asked Khanna for the phone, and told Veer it was an excellent idea, and that he must search right down to the Aglar, along all the paths.

Veer said he would, and that they would start right away if given permission.

I told Khanna this, and being the good policeman that he is, he nodded, and decided to lead the search himself. He told Veer to meet him at the thana in twenty minutes.

Bhabhiji and the saheli returned, faces slightly flushed with the good heat of shared opinions, to overhear this, and now I had to truly take the blame. I was forgiven on one condition. That I would not join the search, and, instead, stay back for a round of more coffee and sweets, and then walk the saheli home.

I had no choice, especially after the amount of dinner I had partaken of.

Khanna's parting comment was, 'Allan, why are you so sure about the need for this search?'

'Instinct,' I replied.

Accepting this as sufficient reason, my good friend the DSP departed, after a prolonged farewell kiss from Bhabhiji. The snow, when Khanna opened the door, welcomed him out into the night with an even colder hug than the one with which it had sent me in.

—

There is something about Mussoorie in the winter.

There are fewer tourists, so the hills seem more intimate. The mood shifts from sombre grey when the clouds are heavy, to hopeful shades of green and gold when the sun sinews through. In the evenings the winter line cuts the sky at the horizon like a crimson sash.

It is a sensual time, a darkening, lonely time, when the soul either burrows deeper into the cave of the senses, to dream and reminisce, or emerges, rekindled, to search for love.

16

I WISH I could say that the evening ended with me and the saheli making passionate love in her cozy little cottage on Camel's Back Road.

It didn't, but it could have (I think!) when I dropped her home in the snow at about 11:30. There was a single light burning inside the cottage, and several lights burning in both of us, but I still had miles to go before I slept, so we embraced each other sweetly outside the front porch, the snow turning shyly away, her light, warm breasts against me promising other sweet times.

—

First of all I wanted to meet Bhandari-kaka before he closed down for the night after the last show, and then I wanted to stay up to meet Khanna and Veer and the search party when they returned. I'd make sure that Rawat had plenty of hot tea waiting for them, so they could relax and tell me in detail where my instincts had led them.

Tea was again on my mind as I jogged through the snow past the Rink and began to climb Kulri, because I was very keen to share a cup with Bhandari-kaka. Which would mean rousing Salim from slumber so that he could work his magic with Anarkali.

When I slipped in through the Rialto entry way, I noticed that a poster for *Andaaz* (the Rajesh Khanna one, of course) was now up, meaning that it would replace *Mughal-e-Azam* on the rerun circuit from Friday—which was the day after tomorrow. I expected to see Chandu there, as the show was not yet over. But a half-asleep unhappy-looking Salim informed me that Chandu had seated the thirteen people who had come to see the last show, and then headed for home, complaining of a headache and requesting Salim to close up things for the night.

My order of two special teas, with lots of sugar, cheered Salim up a little, and I listened to the closing scenes of the film as Salim got Anarkali going—in the canteen, that is. Our song had come and gone, and I asked Salim if the music from the film had awoken him from his half-slumber, and he said, 'Not at all.'

The tea was ready. I took a sip from one of the glasses, expressed my delight to Salim, and then went in to meet Bhandari-kaka.

Kaka, of course, was waiting patiently for me, and his ancient face creased into a thousand smiling lines as I touched his feet after presenting him with the tea.

'Allan-baba, I knew you would eventually come to see me, so I wasn't impatient. What a great, great pleasure to see you!'

He sipped his tea with relish, but his eyes never left me.

'Kaka, I was keeping you for the last, because you are the best.'

'And also, Allan-baba, because you now have nothing left to ask me.'

He raised his glass of tea in tribute, even as the film ended and he turned his attention to the ritual of closing down the projector and winding up the last reel.

I watched him in silence, the frail and gentle old man patiently going about his task with a devotion that was undiminished even after forty-five years and thousands and thousands of shows.

What tribute could I give him? Except a hot glass of tea with plenty of sugar, and and a love that passeth understanding.

His task over, Kaka sat back on his little stool, and he and I talked of days and films gone by, of his grandchildren, of Uttaranchal, of Chandu, of my career, until he quietly pointed out that Khanna and Veer would be back soon from their search.

I had mentioned nothing of the search to Kaka, and we had not spoken at all about the incident of only twenty-four hours ago.

I touched Kaka's feet again, and started to pick up the two glasses, now contentedly empty, to return them to Salim. But Kaka stopped me, saying that Salim must have gone home by now, and that he would return the glasses in the morning.

Properly washed, I was sure.

—

The world would be so much poorer a place without people from my father's generation in it.

They are so wise, and yet they never have to show off their wisdom. They are aware of so much, and yet know so well when to speak and when to remain silent.

And because of this silence, and this quiet wisdom, so many of us younger people forget that they are also full of passion, whether in love or lust or longing.

And the way they speak! What a pleasure it had been to listen to Kaka. Elegant, effortless Hindustani came flowing out, words that I had not heard for decades—phrases and delightful metaphors, tiny twists of syllables which opened sweeping vistas of meaning—

and with those words flowed out equally eloquent thoughts. This is what all languages should really be— no more, and no less, than doors and windows for our thoughts.

17

THERE WERE THREE or four paths which Khanna and Veer and the search party could return by, and I decided to start from the nearest one, and then work my way further out. The snow had lessened, and the roads and paths were paved with a beautiful white, which glowed in the moonlight from a clearing sky.

I wanted to be totally alone in my waiting and my wandering.

And I was. It was delicious, to wander and wonder as the snow crunched underfoot and the moon sang overhead. I, too, began to softly make my way through the scrapbook-litany of my favourite songs, singing not only to myself, but to the saheli and Bhabhiji as well. Not to mention all mankind and the entire universe.

Which was very unusual, because I normally sing only to, and for, myself.

I heard the hustle and bustle of the police party

returning before I saw them. I had walked all the way
to Childers, where the path I expected them to return
by reaches the top of the Landour ridge. They shone
their torches through the night like a dozen Chandus
showing the way to distant rows in an open-air Rialto
made of the hills, and I called out for Khanna when
they came close.

He called back, 'Allan, your instincts were right!
Just see what we have found!'

And what they had found was laid out on the snow
on the Childers path: pieces of black cotton, torn and
bloodstained; a single low-heeled black shoe with its
strap broken; a grey shawl, surprisingly intact, with
clots of blood and some greying hair on it; and the
remains of a satin purse which had been ripped to
shreds.

———

It was Veer who had been carrying this collection, and
Veer who neatly arranged it on the snow in the
moonlight.

Torn cloth, blood stains, small clumps of hair, and
a single shoe.

Khanna reported that the shoe had been found
much higher up, at the top of a steep slope along the
path leading down from the graveyard. The shoe was
in the middle of the road, very plain to see, but the

bushes at the edge of the path overlooking the steep
khud were flattened and broken, as if a heavy object,
or a body, had slipped over the edge.

At the bottom of the slope down which the path
zigzagged, was recovered the bloodstained shawl. It
was against a rock that that had bloodstains on it, too.
The rock was a good two hundred metres straight
down from where the shoe was found, and almost
halfway to the Aglar.

And, most interesting of all, the ground around
where the shawl was found was all scuffed and
scratched, the marks still visible despite the fresh snow.
There also seemed to be a trail—as if something big
had been dragged—right from that point down to the
Aglar. A trail that went straight down, ignoring the
path completely.

Unfortunately, the snow had covered up any clear
footprints, or other prints, but there were drops of
blood here and there on rocks that were above the
snow.

Finally, right down at the bottom, near the Aglar
itself, the bloodstained pieces of black cotton and the
shredded black satin of the purse were found, quite
close together. The snow there was much lighter here,
and there appeared to be animal prints of some kind,
large marks slightly obscured by the snow and the
muddy water at the edge of the Aglar.

After Khanna had explained all this, and told me how Veer had quite daringly followed the drag path down from the rock to the Aglar, everyone looked to me for some kind of explanation.

I, in turn, turned to Veer.

'Sir, we have to check the blood samples of course to be absolutely sure, but the colour of the shawl and the pieces of cloth matches what the lady was wearing. About the shoe we are not so sure, but Bhola had mentioned how she had taken money from a small, black purse to pay for the tickets. And her hair was short, and greying, like the samples on the shawl.'

Khanna, weary from the climb, said, 'Veer, that is all well and good. But what in the world does all this mean?'

'Sir, I have been trying to figure that out all the way up from the Aglar. What I can understand is that the lady, probably fed up with her snoring husband who wouldn't let her enjoy the film—all the others watching the film confirmed that lalaji's snoring was very loud—decided to go for a walk by herself along Camel's Back Road. She took the short cut from the back of Rialto, which is why nobody saw her.'

'Veer, that is also well and good. But to end up on the path below the graveyard? And lose her shoe there?'

'Sir, I can only surmise that the graveyard seemed

a quiet and—sorry for the word—romantic place to wander, so she kept on going down and down until she reached the path, and there she must have slipped because of the heels on her shoes, or maybe one of the straps broke—'

Khanna broke in once again, 'Veer, it all sounds very far-fetched. A woman who has never been to Mussoorie before, finding her way onto Camel's Back Road, and down through the graveyard?'

'Maybe, sir, she had been to Mussoorie before.'

Veer looked to me for support, and I just nodded my head in tentative agreement.

'Right,' carried on Khanna, 'she has been to Mussoorie before, and knows the way down through the graveyard, and then she slips on the path, and falls straight down for about two hundred metres, clutching her shawl, hitting her head on the rocks, and is either knocked unconscious, or dies instantly.'

Heads all around nodded in agreement.

'Then how did she get from there to the banks of the Aglar? And where the hell is the body?'

He turned to me, as did everyone else, so I told them what I thought could have happened, going by the clues they'd picked up.

'Khanna, it's possible—just possible—that her fall disturbed a mother bear and her cubs, and in her anger the bear attacked the lady, who was either dead or unconscious. There are a lot of bears around Mussoorie, especially in the winter months when tourists are fewer, and the residents do not move around as much outside their homes, especially at night.'

The nodding of heads had ceased, and everyone was staring at me with a mixture of confusion and concentration.

At this point, the Garhwali policeman—I think his name is Thapliyal—suddenly followed up on my line of thinking with surprising enthusiasm.

'In that same anger, generated by the mother bear's concern for her cubs, the body was dragged down the slope to the Aglar, where the clothes were torn badly. Then, in a final fit of rage, the mother bear tossed the body into the Aglar, from where it was carried away by the current towards the Jamuna.'

The resulting silence was finally broken by Khanna. 'Allan, do you really think that is possible?'

'What other explanation can we come up with? I mean, we have a very unusual collection of evidence here. And the prints at the Aglar are clearly not human—or so you tell me. Above all, Veer can confirm that for a man to drag the body down the slope from the rock to the Aglar would be impossible. Besides, why would a man do such a thing?'

'And the purse? Ripped to shreds?' persisted Khanna.

I picked up the satin remains of the purse, and had a close look. There were some crumbs stuck in the cloth, and the remains of a wrapper. I tasted the crumbs. Sweet. Chocolaty. The wrapper remains were very, very small, and impossible to identify.

'The cubs,' I stated. 'They attacked the purse to get to the chocolate which was inside.'

This minute piece of evidence turned the tide in favour of the mother-bear theory. Veer was ready to go back down and search the Aglar up to the Jamuna for the body immediately, but the snow was falling thick and fast again, and Khanna told him to wait until the morning.

It was almost 2 a.m. Twenty-four hours since I had called Mussoorie from Chhuttmalpur. A day in a lifetime. A lifetime in a day.

On the way back from Landour to town, driving down those roads as familiar as the veins on the back of our hands, we considered our conclusion carefully. Yes, it was true that in the winter the animals did come very close to the town; and, yes, bears were known to attack people, especially when their cubs were threatened; and, yes, from all reports the lady did look the romantic type who could wander off on her own on a winter's night in Mussoorie.

And slowly, the tragedy of the death—and then the horror of it—began to hit home. We were a very silent group upon returning to the thana, and even Rawat's tea, hot and sweet though it was, warmed only the surface.

—

Sleep is such a marvellous pastime.

Like running, it can still be pure and simple. And, again like running, while fast asleep your mind can drift away into uncharted meadows rimmed by small streams and delicate flowers.

My two favourite times for sleeping are either in the mid-afternoon, between 2 and 4 p.m., with just a bedspread for a covering, and a well-made bed under you to provide the most delicious, most sensual— almost illicit—support; or in the early, early morning, starting from about 3 a.m., when you know you don't have to get up until at least 9.

Add two other very important factors to these timings, and you have attained nirvana—first, the sleep must be well earned; second, it must end with a nice, hot cup of tea served by a lovely lady.

18

AND IT WAS at 9 a.m. that I awoke the next morning, warmly ensconced in a razai, a speciality of the Khanna household, whether in the main bedroom, or the guest room.

I sat up and pulled back the curtain to see a world white with snow, and more snow on the way. Even Veer wouldn't venture out to the Aglar in that weather.

Bhabhiji knocked on the door, lovingly calling out that she had brought tea for me and didn't I appreciate how much she cared for me. All this was said in mock imitation of the saheli's voice. I got out of bed, dragging the razai behind me, and opened the door, to be rewarded with the sight of an absolutely sumptuous-looking Bhabhiji, hair all asunder, pink-and-blue nightgown recklessly covered with a tiny shawl, holding a steaming cup of tea in her plump, fair hand.

But before she actually gave me the cup, she

demanded a full report on all of last night's post-dinner activities—which I promised to give, provided she reciprocated in kind!

Oh, what a snowfall of laughter followed, which even brought Khanna running from the living room, morning paper in hand.

Thus began my second day in Mussoorie, and by the time I actually made it out of the warmth of Bhabhiji and her breakfast, I found that all of Mussoorie, needing no morning newspaper whatsoever, was abuzz with the news of last night's search.

The sun had now begun to sparkle on the snowdrifts, which were well over my waist up against the walls. It was great fun reaching Rialto—floundering through the drifts, and fending off snowball attacks from mischievous schoolboys.

From the conversations overheard along the way, Veer was decidedly the hero of the search, followed closely by Khanna, who was greatly appreciated because, being such a senior officer, he still spent half the night in the snow, leading his men all the way to the Aglar and back.

I was mentioned as a source of inspiration, but that was all.

I scurried into the warmth of Arora-sahib's office, where at least seven other people were already cocooned. I was greeted with backslapping and congratulations, until I had to remind everyone that a lady had died, and a husband had to be informed.

A task that came my way by duty, and by choice.

I called lalaji in Delhi from Arora-sahib's office, but he was not at home. Then I spent nearly fifteen minutes trying to get through on his mobile, finally succeeding when the second round of tea was on its way.

Lalaji said he would call back immediately.

Which he did. The conversation was short and businesslike. Lalaji accepted everything that I said, and agreed that there was no hope of finding his wife alive, not after two nights and a day. He enquired about the body, which I said we would keep searching for.

He sighed, and said that if the body had reached the Jamuna, then his wife's soul would find peace. And even if the body didn't reach the Jamuna, it had mingled with waters that eventually reached the Sangam.

I murmured that I understood. He thanked me for my efforts. There were no apparent signs of guilt or grief, and I would been surprised to find any in a man like him. I'd met him only once, but I was certain I'd figured him out.

I told him that the blood samples were being checked today, but that I had no doubt that they would match the type that his doctor in Delhi had told me yesterday over the phone.

Lalaji agreed, thanked me once again, and said, in parting, that he would have come to Mussoorie to thank everyone, but now the memories in Mussoorie were just too sad to face.

Again I said I understood, and promised to see him in Delhi upon my return.

And that was the end of the conversation with lalaji.

The group said that I had handled it well. When I conveyed lalaji's last message about wanting to return to Mussoorie to thank everyone but not feeling up to it, things became sombre for a while as every man present was silenced by sympathy, and it seemed the best possible end to a sad saga.

I said I would return to Delhi tomorrow morning, which brought from a suddenly cheerful Arora-sahib the following comment: 'And what will you do for the rest of the day? Visit Camel's Back Road?'

It is no wonder that Bhabhiji is lovingly known as 'All-India Radio' in Mussoorie.

I blushed a little, pretended to shoot Arora-sahib through the heart, and leant back in my chair, closing my eyes.

'I have two things on my agenda—first, a nap from 2 to 4 p.m.; and then, after a big *khana*, I want to see the last show of *Mughal-e-Azam* with Chandu.'

'With Chandu?' asked Arora-sahib. 'What do you mean, with Chandu?'

As a fresh round of aloo-tikkis arrived, I replied, 'Yes, Arora-sahib, with Chandu. I want tonight to be a farewell for Chandu. After all, how long can he go on checking tickets at Rialto? Till his other eye also develops a permanent squint? Let's give him a big dinner at Neelams, a little to drink, and then, Arora-sahib, you stand at the Rialto door and check our tickets while Chandu and I go in to see the film!'

It was amazing to see the enthusiasm with which my idea was greeted. I had obviously struck a chord in everyone's hearts, and immediately plans were under way, ranging from a retirement gift and the opening of Chandu's Provident Fund, to the type of drinks to be ordered, to what Chandu's favourite dishes were, and, finally, to what Arora-sahib should say in his farewell tribute to Chandu.

How different would it have been, I wonder, had they known what I knew.

No one thought to ask Chandu what he thought about all this. The timing was perfect, the mood was perfect, the cause was perfect. Bhola would find another young man from Chandu's village to take Chandu's place, and that would make Chandu happy. No more questions.

Then, as everybody realized that Chandu would be leaving, the Chandu stories began, the Chandu jokes were told, anecdotes about a favourite friend or brother exchanged like boxes of sweets at Diwali. And memories of him began to fill the intimate confines of Arora-sahib's office.

Soon afterwards, I went in search of the man concerned.

Not to tell him of all the surprises in store for him, but to personally invite him to see the movie with me. And it was on that walk that I remembered it was Thursday, and that *Andaaz* would take over from *Mughal-e-Azam* tomorrow.

—

There is a time and a place for almost everything.

And when that time and that place are perfect, the rhythm and rhyme of the universe move in harmony, and we mere mortals are blessed to be part of the music.

19

I THOUGHT IT would be easy to find Chandu, but this time I was wrong.

He wasn't around Rialto, nor on Kulri, nor towards the Ropeway—and it was much too early for him to be visiting the 'green curtain'.

I returned to Rialto from my search, to be told by Salim that Chandu had been spotted near the Cemetery gate on Camel's Back Road. I took the short cut behind Rialto which leads to Camel's Back Road, and headed towards the Cemetery, the snow already worn down on the main part of the road.

Chandu was standing in a patch of sun, smoking a bidi, looking out across the Aglar valley.

He must have heard me coming, but, like yesterday morning at my uncle's bench, he didn't react until I was close and called his name. This time, however, Chandu turned towards me with the most amazing look in his eyes—a look I had never seen before. A

look of vulnerability, a questioning look, almost like a child's. Questions not like the ones I had fled from on the plains, but driven by a much deeper search.

I could only answer by embracing him, once again. And even as I did so now, I knew that Chandu's company, even Mussoorie, so full of memories of simpler times, was only a temporary resting place, not the final destination.

When we had both relaxed just a little, I said, 'Chandu, I'm going back to Delhi tomorrow morning. And before I go—tonight—I want to see the last show of *Mughal-e-Azam* with you. For old time's sake. Do you realize that you and I have never actually sat in Rialto together and watched a film?'

There were so many things Chandu could have said in reply to my offer, but all he said was, 'Sahib, it will be an honour. No, not only an honour. But a great pleasure as well.'

We stood together there in the patch of sun on the snowy Camel's Back Road, the gate of the Cemetery a solitary witness. I asked Chandu for a bidi.

'But you never smoked, Sahib!'

'Today I feel like it.'

I tried to smoke the bidi the way Chandu does, wrapping both hands around it, but only succeeded in burning my hand. Chandu, almost chuckling, showed me how it is done.

When the first wave of smoke hit my throat, I

coughed, but bravely struggled on. Chandu pounded me on the back, and said, 'Sahib, it is a habit you have to get used to.'

The patch of sun disappeared, and shadows seemed to lengthen slightly. But the two of us were together.

'Chandu, Arora-sahib is very keen to see you as soon as possible. Some sort of surprise. He's waiting in his office.'

This time when Chandu turned to look at me, the vulnerability and questioning lingered only in the corners of his eyes.

—

As the years roll by, there are certain things we do—or abstain from doing—which form our character.

We do these things—or don't do them—almost as a reflex action, without any deep thought or consideration. Then, at a certain age, we are given a moment, a brief opportunity, to confront and either accept or challenge these decisions, the pattern we have fallen into. To look at them in the light of new wisdom, new understanding.

If we recognize this moment, if we seize the fleeting opportunity, we can discard what we don't like about ourselves, and keep what we do. It is not half as easy as a snake shedding its skin, but it can be done.

And if we are lucky, we will have kept the spirit alive deep inside.

20

MY AFTERNOON NAP would have done my father proud. Buried deep in the razai, I dreamt of small, roly-poly boys cuddling up to pipe-smoking fathers. I heard temple bells ringing from the evening's forests; I saw brothers playing cricket in the front lawns, until slim and smiling mothers called them in for lunch (usually colour coordinated), and sisters being teased mercilessly and yet loved and admired deeply. Then I sensed childhood disappear beyond some boundary, and elegant women with wise, shimmering eyes beckoned to me, urging me, gently, to grow up.

I was awoken, for the second time that day, by Bhabhiji's voice offering me tea. And samosas. It was 4 p.m., and sense and order prevailed. With just a dash of masala.

By the time I finished the tea and three samosas, Khanna was back from the office, and the winter line was becoming visible over the Doon Valley. I had to have one more samosa with Khanna as he told me that the preparations for Chandu's farewell were in full swing. An early dinner at Neelams, starting at 8 p.m., followed by a small ceremony at 9 p.m. at Rialto, when Arora-sahib would check the tickets at the door, and Chandu and I would be escorted to the seats I had specifically requested. There would be speeches and gifts in Chandu's honour. (Khanna couldn't stop laughing as he described Arora-sahib practicing his Chandu squint, right eye closed over an imaginary torch!)

'There was a feeling in the town that in view of the tragedy, drinking and merriment should be kept to the minimum. But everyone is in favour of the farewell.'

The winter line was at her scarlet best, and the evening lingered on to admire her.

'There are drinks for a select few—including Chandu—in Arora-sahib's office at 7 p.m. Which is only an hour away.'

'And Chandu?' I asked. 'Did he agree to all this?'

'Almost immediately. Especially since he knew you would be here tonight, and gone tomorrow.'

Here tonight, gone tomorrow.

Like a rerun at Rialto.

—

'*Zindagi, kaisi hai paheli—*'

The riddle of life, indeed.

21

ARORA-SAHIB'S CHANDU act was the highlight of the evening, and would have been a smashing success even if not preceded by the best of drinks, the best of food, and the best of fellowship.

Most of Mussoorie was there, and Rialto hadn't been so full in decades.

As a squinting Arora-sahib led Chandu and me to our seats, there was a great round of applause. Chandu had held back his tears so far, but upon seeing the seat numbers, he held my arm and began to weep.

Jot Singh gave a marvellous speech in praise of Chandu, in which he stated that Chandu was as much a landmark of Mussoorie as the Rink and the Clock Tower and Camel's Back and Rialto itself, and that whenever Chandu wanted to return for a visit, he would get a free meal at Neelams, and a free ticket to the show at Rialto.

Another round of applause for Chandu—also

because Jot Singh had kept his speech so short—and then the film began. But not before Bhandari-kaka, from the projection booth, led a cheer of 'Chandu, zindabad! Chandu, zindabad!'

The lights were dimmed, and then the voyage into the past was under way. It was the culmination of an old bond—between the film and Chandu and me; and when, at the interval, Salim brought us tea (free of charge, as he laughingly told Chandu), the three of us, after Salim left, were together in silence. The rest of the crowd, sensing the moment, left us in peace. Less than ten minutes later, *Mughal-e-Azam* spoke again, rich and reckless and passionate.

About five minutes before the song started, I slipped away. I was as quiet as possible, and I don't think Chandu noticed.

Moments later, Chandu did the same thing, and came to the small patch of grass under the tree behind Rialto—the small patch of grass that, forty years ago, had been a small *maidan* with an unobstructed view, out across Camel's Back Road, of the Aglar valley.

Chandu stood almost directly under the tree, where there was still a small, grassy slope, and lit a bidi, wrapping his hands around it. He looked at ease, but at the same time very much at attention, like a veteran hunter sensing game at hand.

Just then, our song started, and the volume suddenly increased dramatically.

Rafi had never sounded better.

Even as Chandu turned towards Rialto in wonder, I spoke from the tree above him, 'It was I who gave tea to Bhandari-kaka tonight.'

And then I jumped down from the tree, landing next to Chandu, slipping only slightly in the snow.

—

'*Jab pyar kiya, to darna kya?*'

Having chosen love, what do we fear?

So often in life, the simplicity of that challenge is as close to our truth as words can get.

22

'IT WAS PAUL, not me, who had climbed this tree forty years ago, and watched you and her together, with the song playing in the background. Only Paul had the guts to do such a thing—skip out of the hostel late on a Saturday night, sneak into town, see the film and also spy on our hero.'

Chandu stood silent and still.

'I could never have done it, couldn't have imagined anyone doing it, which is probably why I didn't believe Paul when he told me the whole story.'

Rafi's voice, now as then, was the only witness. And that voice seemed to flow deeper and richer in appreciation.

'Maybe that is why I became a policeman, and Paul a businessman.'

Now the orchestra soared to the heavens, and the night was filled with hope and strength.

Chandu was looking deep into me, not searching

for the truth, but now fully realizing it. His squint seemed to disappear for a moment. Then he cupped his hands around the bidi, drew it to his face, and taking in the smoke, spoke like the Chandu I love so much— simple and straight. 'But sahib, what you have done for me would make even Paul very, very proud.'

'I have only done what I had to do, Chandu—what I was destined to do, ever since you showed me my first film at Rialto, ever since you met me yesterday morning at my uncle's bench.'

'Sahib, please don't misunderstand me. I knew that the only person in the world who could understand, who could solve—'

'Was me. And how right you were, Chandu. As always. You knew it, you felt it. That is why you were waiting at my uncle's bench, convinced that I would return. That is why you sang our song out to the mist and the hills.'

'But sahib, it was not a scheme on my part, not a trap, I took a chance, I just hoped—I believed—that you would come, after all those years. Sometimes, sahib, all you can do is to have faith.'

'I know, Chandu, I know. If it had been a scheme or a trap, it never would have worked. It wouldn't have been you and me. And if you had simply told me the story straight, I would never have been moved to do what I did. It could only have been a chance. You had to take the risk. You and I, Chandu, we are sportsmen who love to play the game by certain rules— not only of the book, but of the spirit, too. Our meeting at my uncle's bench yesterday morning was as natural as the sun rising over the Haunted House.'

Our song would not last much longer, but tonight no one had to rush back into Rialto when the song ended.

While the magic lasted, Chandu spoke from his heart. 'Sahib, I knew that you would do something. But this? Risking your entire career, your entire reputation? You have never told a lie in your whole life.'

Rafi's voice was reaching its crescendo, so I gestured to Chandu, and listened in silence. It was the only reply I could make.

Then the song ended, Bhandari-kaka turned down the volume (I could see him smiling to himself), and Chandu and I cleared places in the snow for the two of us to sit. Chandu offered me a bidi, but I declined the offer, saying that it wasn't a habit quite yet.

There we sat, two ageing men in the snow, as our film ran its final rerun at Rialto.

'Getting the right length and colour of hair was a real problem, Chandu. Finally I stole some from Bhabhiji's hairbrush in her bathroom. This I did even before Rawat told me his tale of the torch.'

There was a faint murmur of dialogues coming out from Rialto.

'I thought for a moment you were on to me, Chandu, when you caught me outside of the 'green curtain' with the bottle of blood from LCH in my pocket—my type is the same as hers—and the bundles of shopping—the shoes and the satin and cotton cloth and the shawl.'

Chandu laughed. 'That explains it. That drama you did with Arora-sahib about getting married. It didn't sound like you at all.'

I chuckled in reply. 'You never know, Chandu.'

It was so comforting—so comfortable—to just talk about everything.

'And you should have seen me, Chandu, sliding head over heels down that slope towards the Aglar, dragging two big rocks wrapped up in the cotton cloth, pretending that I was a mother bear! You would have died laughing!'

Chandu just shook his head in wonder, and, like a little schoolboy, I was thrilled for a moment. 'Sahib, you thought of everything!'

'Of course, Bhola's telling me that the lady had demanded only seats A-16 and A-17, and that you had told him to never, ever sell those seats to anyone when *Mughal-e-Azam* was showing, had really got my instincts going inside me. And then when I heard our song

coming from the servants' quarters at Suncliff, and I
charged along the Eyebrow to reach there before the
song ended, Paul's story came back to me as clearly as
the Haunted House emerging from the mists. And I
knew, for certain, at last, that it was true.'

'Just see, sahib, how it was meant to be.'

'Yes, Chandu, it was meant to be. For both of us.'

I leaned back against the slope, closed my eyes, and
said, 'Now, Chandu, now—I want to hear your story.
From you. My instincts are weary from piecing it
together. I want to be the audience now. In A-16.'

Chandu looked at me from his good eye, then
turned away.

'Chandu, our song, it is over. Our film will be over
soon, too. But that is well and good.'

Our shoulders touched, and the snow seemed to be
lessening, just a little.

'We are old men now, Chandu. Everyone will
know that we are sitting and talking about the days
gone by. No one will bother us.'

There was a look of absolute peace on Chandu's
face.

—

The night was cold and sharp. And all was deep, and
dark, and mysterious.

'ALLAN-BABA, WHEN she came into Rialto that night, with her husband trailing behind her, and held out the tickets for A-16 and A-17 towards me, the old torch which she had given me forty years ago shook in my hand as the light swept up from the ticket numbers to her face. I couldn't stare at her for too long, but one glance was enough. She was as beautiful as ever, she was back, and I knew that she was still mine.

'And I, Allan-baba, like an old fool, was all squinted down over the torch, my back bent and my hand shaking, while she turned to her complaining husband and lovingly requested him to understand.

'She was back, Allan-baba! Back to me, back to Rialto, with Bhandari-kaka just starting our film!

'I took them to A-16 and A-17 as calmly as possible, and even asked the husband whether he would like a cup of tea. He said "No" quite rudely—but he is not a bad man, Allan-baba, I know it. He is just one of those men who has been caught up in the business of making money since he was a boy. He knows nothing else.

'When the film started, I stood behind the curtain at the entrance nearest to them, and watched her as the beam from Kaka's projector brightened and dimmed.

'Her hair was cut in the same style as forty years ago. She was in a black salwar-kameez, just as she was on that late summer afternoon in 1960 when she came with her three sahelis to see the first show of *Mughal-e-Azam* at Rialto. The same little purse, too, and the same low-heeled shoes. The only difference was a shawl to keep her warm. A grey shawl, which suited her, and the mood of the night, perfectly.

'She didn't turn to look at me, but then, she didn't have to. She knew I was watching her—I, the old fool, with squinted eye and about seven hundred rupees in my State Bank account. Still checking tickets at Rialto, forty years later.

'Her husband fell asleep, well before the interval. His head fell against her shoulder, and she made no effort to wake him. Then his snoring started. She lifted his head to wake him once, probably thinking that a change of angle might lower the volume of his snoring. But no such luck.

'So she just kept on watching the film, with a look of total concentration, his head upon her shoulder.

'The lights coming on at the interval hardly disturbed the husband's sleep, and I decided not to try and give them tea. Instead, I went to Salim, collected the special tea I had ordered, and went to see Kaka.

'Allan-baba, it was so beautiful when I gave Kaka the tea. He immediately understood. I didn't have to tell him anything. After forty years, Allan-baba! In fact, even then I didn't have to tell Kaka anything—only the first time, when I said the tea was my way of thanking him for raising the volume when our song came on.

'I have never been sure if Kaka knows the whole story. Maybe he does, maybe he doesn't. But he understands.

'When the second half started, I came down from the projection room, and returned to my place behind the curtain. She didn't seem to notice. She was totally involved in the film.

'Just as she used to be for three shows a day—three, six, and nine—for all the six days she stayed in Mussoorie when *Mughal-e-Azam* was released in the summer of 1960.

'You see, Allan-baba, when she came walking up to me on that first day in the afternoon, with her three sahelis in tow, I was discussing football with a friend, and didn't notice her until she held out the tickets for A-16, 17, 18 and 19, and asked me if they were good seats. When I heard her voice, I forgot all about football . . .

'Allan-baba, her voice hasn't changed. When she was requesting her husband the other night to understand, her voice captured me all over again. A softness, a sweetness. No affectation, no hesitation. Aware of its beauty, Allan-baba, and yet not carried away by that beauty.

'Just like her eyes . . . When I looked into them for the first time, they accepted me. They accepted me as the man they loved. At first sight.

'It was my voice that hesitated as I tried to say, "Yes, they are good seats. Right at the back."

'And when she returned for the evening show, with only one saheli and two tickets—A-16 and 17 of course—I barely managed to say, "I hope you liked the seats."

'And when she came back for the night show, with the same saheli and the same tickets, she asked me, "Do you like the film?"

'That was it, Allan-baba. The poor saheli fell asleep in the night show, as I watched from behind that same curtain. But it was 1960, and no young girl could go out alone, especially a young girl from one of the richest families in Delhi.

'Our fingers touched when I checked the tickets for the evening show on the second day. Then I don't know what came over me. I purchased the tickets for the night show before they arrived, and wrote on the

back of her ticket, A-16, "When that song starts—
Zindabad, zindabad—aei mohabbat zindabad!—meet
me behind Rialto." I gave her the ticket in such a way
that she couldn't help noticing what I had written.

'I was standing beneath the tree when the song
started. Bhandari-kaka had his tea, and as she walked
towards me in the darkness, the volume came up. We
just stood there, she and I, under the tree, for as long
as the song lasted. We didn't say a word. Just stood
and looked at each other and listened to our song. At
that time there were hardly any buildings around, so it
was dark under the tree, and we felt totally alone in
our little world.

'The next evening, without any message from me,
she came to me again. Just as she would every evening
and night show for as long as she stayed in Mussoorie,
which was another four days, which meant another
eight cups of tea for Kaka, and another eight meetings
for us.

'Allan-baba, how can I describe that love?

'The song lasts for only about five minutes, which
left very little time to talk. Which was fine with us.
Words were hard to find anyway. We just kept looking
at each other, kept listening to our song. On the second
to last evening, we held hands. During the night show,
we actually sat down, and I put an arm around her
shoulders, and told her of my village across the Aglar,

and the path leading down from the Cemetery, down and across the Aglar, and then up to my village.

'In those days, one could almost see the lights of my village from behind Rialto. She snuggled closer. That was, as I said, on the second to last night.

'On the last evening, she told me of her family in Delhi, and her father's booming jewellery business— and that she had to return to Delhi the next day. That night, when our song ended, she kissed my cheek, pressed a brand new torch into my hand as a farewell present, and, before running off, promised to come back to me.

'Oh, Allan-baba, how beautiful she looked, in her black salwar kameez, running back into the lights of Rialto, her low-heeled shoes clip-clopping in perfect rhythm, her satin purse bouncing at her side, her short, full hair flying around her slim, wonderful neck.

'She promised me that night, Allan-baba. And she kept her promise. She came back. To me.

'Night before last I was waiting under the tree. There are so many buildings around now, and so many more lights. But the tree is still here, and this small patch of grass. I waited in the shadow of the tree, slightly worried about my bad eye and my age. But she walked right up to me, even as Kaka performed his magic. She walked right up to me, and stopped, just a few feet away.

'Allan-baba, I could have died. She is still so beautiful.

'Then she spoke my name, "Chandu." With that same voice, that same truth, that same love. I could face her with courage now, and as her arms reached out to me—for me—lifting the grey shawl, I tried to smile.

'And then her hands touched my face, my eyes— the eye that has gone bad. Allan-baba, the look in her eyes! It was like—it was like—nothing else on earth. I felt as if the whole universe existed just for me.

'Then we were in each other's arms. I felt her slender body against mine for the first time. We were weeping for joy, even as she begged forgiveness. Forgiveness for what, I asked, as the aroma of her hair, her breath filled my senses. You promised that you would come back to me, and you have.

' "But, Chandu—I married and lived with my husband for almost all of these forty years."

'As our song soared in the background, I simply told her that life is not a film. I knew forty years ago that it would be impossible for her to resist her parents' demands that she marry someone from their caste, their circle, someone as rich as them. I still know that today.

' "But Chandu, you never married," she said. "I know that without your telling me. You waited for me

& GENERAL MERCH
RIALTO
Cinema
FIRST TIME IN MUSSOORIE
Daily 3 Shows
3-00 p.m.
6-00 p.m.
9-00 p.m.
MUGAL-E-AZAM
Classic of Immortal Love

for forty years. You are so much stronger than me."

' "No," I said. "I am not stronger. I merely waited. That is much easier."

'I ran my fingers through her soft, greying hair. "You are the strong one," I told her, "you had a promise to fulfil, and you fulfilled it."

'As I spoke those words, our song faded away, and I knew already what to do. I gave her the torch—our torch—and explained to her how to take the short cut down to Camel's Back Road, and then how to get to the Cemetery gate, and to the path leading down to the Aglar. I kissed her hair, and told her to start right away, before the film ended. And I told her not to worry about anything, to keep singing our song, to believe that love was truly eternal.

'She nodded, and looked so serene when she turned away that I almost let her go on her own. All the way down through the Cemetery and across the Aglar and up to my village, where my mother was still waiting for her *bahu*.

'It would have been the perfect ending to the perfect film.

'But, as I said, I know that life is not a film. So I quietly called her back, and told her that Bhola would meet her at the Cemetery gate in ten minutes, and he would lead her to my village. Again she nodded, this time with a smile, and then was off, taking small steps through the snow.

'Bhola lives just across from Rialto, and he is usually at home, unless off at Library with his lady-love. Fortunately he was home, and he understood everything immediately, and ran off, moving so well, to meet her at the Cemetery gate.

'And Bhola was back by very early morning, because he runs so swiftly. I was waiting for him at Childers, the path I had told him to return by. He told me that she is a great walker and that they had reached my village, safe and sound, in less than three hours, and that my mother had welcomed her with a loving embrace, no questions asked.

'Allan-baba, a man's village is his true home. No one from my village will ever tell anybody in Mussoorie about what happened. I know that.

'Now, Allan-baba, I have one confession to make. Bhola would never, ever have informed you about the tickets she asked for—A-16 and 17—unless I told him to. He is from my village, and I am his elder. Telling him to tell you about the tickets was the only little bit of scheming I had to do. Bhola himself thought up the excuse of visiting his ladylove at Library to cover his not being in Mussoorie that night after the show.

'Am I forgiven, Allan-baba?'

I had drifted far, far away as I listened to Chandu's tale, and I returned, cleansed and healed, to punch him lightly on the arm.

'Then, Chandu, you ran from Childers to my uncle's bench to meet me there, because you knew that is where I would return to first of all, because you knew that this little baba would prove that "*Zindabad, zindabad—aei mohabbat zindabad!*" is even more true in life than in a film.'

'And you did, sahib,' said Chandu. 'Sometimes, if you have faith, things just have to work out.'

For people like you, Chandu, I said to myself—for people who have kept the faith. That is what I learnt from you, from my return to Mussoorie. We must keep the faith.

'Now, Chandu, there is only one, final scene left. Here, take this torch I bought for you—the same one I used yesterday evening on my descent to the Aglar. Go home. She's waiting for you.'

As I handed him the torch, still shiny and new, Chandu lowered his head. I knew he wanted to touch my feet—not as a formality, but as the truest gesture of love he knew.

I held him by the shoulders, and slowly he straightened up.

We were face to face, with only the lightly falling snow between us.

His squinted eye shone in the moonlight, and the tilt of his head was poised and perfect.

Then he was gone.

—

I fulfilled my promise, and went and met the husband in Delhi.

He was not in mourning, but he allowed that now that his wife was no more, he truly appreciated her for the first time.

They had produced no children—the husband admitted that the medical problem was his, not hers—so life was now only business and more business. This he said as his mobile rang incessantly, and he excused himself to attend to it.

I slipped away, marvelling at the wonders of love.

The old Jawa started at the first kick, and a new song was already forming in my heart as I made my way out into the Delhi traffic.